Night's Dew

PUBLISHED BY LULU ENTERPRISES, INC.
KCL CREATIVE WRITING SOCIETY
King's College London Student Union, Macadam Building,
Surrey Street, London WC2R 2NS
http://www.kclcreativewriting.com
© KCL Creative Writing Society 2014
First edition.

All works in this anthology are the intellectual property of their named authors.

This anthology is comprised of works of fiction. Names and characters are the product of the authors' imagination and any resemblance to actual persons, living or dead, is entirely coincidental.

This book is sold subject to the condition that is shall not, by way of trade or otherwise, be lent, resold, hired out or otherwise circulated without the writers' prior consent in any form of binding or cover other than that in which it is published and without similar condition including this condition being imposed on the subsequent purchaser.

Cover illustration by Argula Rublack

Typeset by Hussain Ajina

ISBN: 978-1-326-07175-2

Night's Dew

KCL Creative Writing Society 2011-2012
King's College London Student Union

Contents

Foreword	11
The Silence by *Emily Nelson*	14
Not Every Writer's Dream by *Mirjana Govedarica*	16
Imaginings by *Navleen Kalsi*	34
Polygamy and Other Metaphysical Problems by *Hussain Ajina*	36
The Substance of Dust by *Argula Rublack*	52
Dream Story by *Anissa Putois*	74
The Exaphanisis by *Agamemnon Apostolou*	82
Three First Pages of Unwritten Novels by *David Lowry*	104

We are literary lions. Hear us roar.

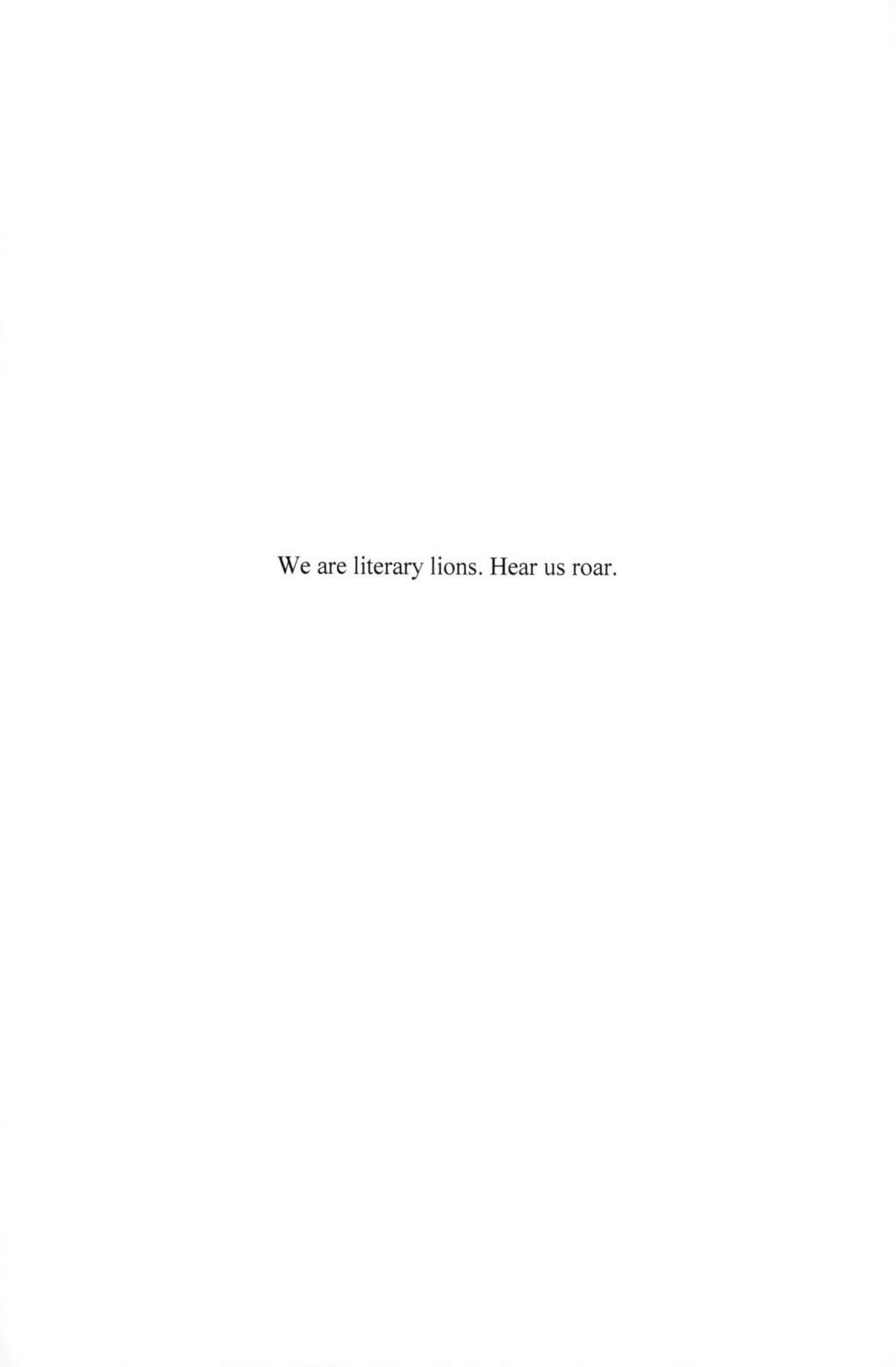

Foreword
The Omnipotence of Dreams

I have taken the subtitle of this foreword from André Breton's *First Manifesto of Surrealism*, in which he stated that, amongst other things, a belief in the omnipotence of dreams lies at the very heart of surrealism. What drew Breton and his fellow surrealists so inexorably to the world of dreams is plain enough; for the surrealist, fascinated as he or she is by pure psychic automatism, there can be no higher mode of being than that of dreams, where the mind takes leave of its owner's will and creates fantastical realities all of its own accord. It's perhaps this quality that drew us to dreams as the theme for this anthology.

Dreams are, for us, the ultimate in psychic experience. In our dreams we thunder below unfathomed deeps, or huddle away, entombed by idyllic bowers, or soar amongst titanic, sunlit clouds. In all cases we terrorform the waking world to the contours of our particular psyches. Dreams are the only glimpses we get of the other side of our minds, little globules of wonder clinging onto our memories. They are glowing pinpricks of light in a sunless sky, like the moon and stars of our souls, or, as we have decided to dub them, the night's dew.

Our contributors have been very free with the idea of 'dreams' as a theme for this anthology. Some chose to interpret the theme literally, as the psychedelic trips we take while sleeping, whilst others chose to think of 'dreams' in the sense of the hopes and aspirations that very often form the core of our waking lives, and more than a couple exploited both meanings of the word. The single concept that cropped up again and again, however, was the idea of dreams turned to reality. Perhaps we shouldn't find this too surprising, though.

As creative writers, isn't that precisely the business in which we find ourselves? Can there really be any more apt metaphor (is it even a metaphor?) for literary expression than the physical manifestation of dreams? In that light the processes of dreaming and of writing are strikingly similar. In both cases we endeavour to represent our thoughts and feelings in some kind of coherent, tangible structure; in dreams to ourselves and in literature to everyone else. In our nights we bear witness to our unclothed souls, rendered in an invented world of dreams. In our days we drag this world across sheets of paper, manifested at last in the magic of words. Here are our dreams then, glistening in the daylight for all the world to see.

Hussain Ajina
President, 2012

The Silence
Emily Nelson

I have never heard the Silence behind
The unceasing hum of cars that whisper
and whirr through my window, pressing my mind
Into shapes of pipes and prattling people.
Ticking. Wind creeps coldly through cloudy panes
And clinging fingers grasp echoes of thoughts
unnoticed. Intangible as the grains
of time, rushing through glass and outstretched palms.

Crowned with crunching paper and quiet breath
The Silence possesses its solitude
And I mine. In the clamouring distress
I contemplate the creatures of my mind.
Or yours. Inside the two they hide, outside
They wink from walls in hues of cream and beige
As if all the world of colour had died,
And left behind institutional grey.

The Silence stamps its solid existence
Onto listening minds, marooned within
the ties of ticking, the prat'ling pretence
Of uniqueness, uniform delusions.
Pressing purposefully within the zones
Where we become a self, in flickering
Electrics and the quiet of alone
The Silence remains as a reminder.

Not Every Writer's Dream
Mirjana Govedarica

Cora found herself in the middle of a dense patch of trees, with no idea where she was or how she came to be there. Sunlight broke through the dense atmosphere in shards of pale yellow, but did little to diffuse the heavy scent of damp earth and rotting leaves around her. She was breathing hard, as though she had been running, but she could not recall the chase. It was as though someone had thrown her headlong into the middle of events and left her to fend for herself in the unusual new environment. Yelling echoed in the distance. Instinctively, she broke into a run.

The forest rushed past her as she trampled through her surroundings. Although she broke every twig and stamped on every dry leaf beneath her feet, Cora met very little resistance from the trees she hurtled past. Something in the depths of her subconscious told her that she should have tripped and fallen by now. The undergrowth was too thick with roots and she was too unskilled for her to have lasted this long without sustaining an injury. It was as though the forest was nothing more than a movie reel playing in the background of her chase. Everything was too clean and clear.

She let herself slow down and switched to a brisk walk, sensing a change in the atmosphere. As her blind panic began to evaporate, Cora realised that the yelling had died down. The area around her was quiet; only the rustle of the wind through the trees could be heard. It was lighter here. There was more space for her to move and whole patches of sunlight broke through the leafy canopy above. *Perhaps the noise was nothing more than a hunter's call,* she thought as she stepped over a particularly thick knot of roots. *Perhaps...*

Cora froze. She had reached what appeared to be the very edge of the forest. Through the frame of trees ahead of her, she could see a familiar piece of stonework. It was the intricate border of a set of wide iron gates she had never expected to see. Cora now knew exactly where she was. It was a place she had been dreaming and writing about for years; her small piece of fantasy was now standing only a few feet away from her, as real as the book in your hands. She moved hesitantly towards it, protected by the cover of the trees. There, guarded by armed knights, stood the entrance to the Star City.

"Who goes there?" called the knight standing closest to her, reacting sharply to the cracking twig as Cora moved closer to get a better look. She recoiled, ducking back into the shadows of the forest. An unexplainable nervousness had settled in her stomach. Now that she had to face her characters, Cora was glad that she had kept clothing simple. Her dark trousers and grey jacket were not very different from that of the guardian on patrol. She pushed up her sleeves and took a deep breath before marching into the sunlit clearing. "Identify yourself."

Cora blinked. The guard stared down at her with dark blue eyes, a trademark of citizens from the city. The familiar, angular face of one of her lead characters was unmistakable.

"Alexander Orion," she murmured, unable to stop herself. His professional poise faltered for a moment and a shadow passed across his face.

"What did you say?" he snapped.

"N-nothing," Cora replied hastily. "I'm just a traveller. My name is Cora Sands and I would like to see your city."

Alexander frowned, clearly suspicious.

"If you're *just a traveller*, how is it that you're carrying no luggage?" he retorted.

Her gaze dropped to her feet, thinking quickly. *It was a fair point...*

"I was robbed by bandits," she said. "They stole everything I had and left me alone in the middle of the forest, with no means to find my way."

17

"You're looking particularly clean after a robbery and escapade through the forest," Alexander observed. It was her fault for writing him as such a sharp and dedicated guardsman. Of course, it had never occurred to her that one day she would have to get past him.

"I had to take care of myself, now that this is all I own," Cora explained slowly. "I let them take everything without a fight, on the condition that they didn't harm me."

There was a long pause.

"There are no bandits in this area of the country," he said.

It was true. She had never had reason to think about the outlying regions of the city, so she had written a high defence system for the region surrounding the gates and left it at that. In reality, there was nothing in the forest but animals and the people who hunted them for market days. Another long silence had fallen between them as Alexander waited for her response. Cora shifted nervously on the spot, transferring her weight from one foot to the other as she tried to think of a new explanation for her arrival. It was difficult to explain to a fictional character that everything around them was a dream, particularly when she had so little experience with dreams of this level of vivacity.

"I think you need to come with me, miss," Alexander said in a grave voice. He took her by the arm and pulled her in the direction of a heavily guarded pair of doors to the left of the main entrance. Cora panicked and tried to pull her arm free. She knew what lay behind those doors; a long, dark path that would lead them directly to the dungeons beneath the palace.

"No really, it's fine," she insisted, still struggling to pull herself free from his grip. "I'll go somewhere else… I don't have to see the city!"

"Your behaviour has been deemed suspicious," he explained, apparently unaffected by her attempt to break free. "All you need to do is answer a few questions for us."

Cora snorted in disbelief.

"Really, I promise I'll-"

His grip on her arm slipped and she stumbled backwards. There, imprinted on her forearm where Alexander had been holding her, was a dense pattern of intricate letters. The knight had also stopped to stare at the markings. Careful to keep her distance from him, Cora brought her arm up to her eyes for closer inspection. It took her a second to recognise her own handwriting and the sight of Alexander's old character notes. Although it had been a long time since she had seen them, the words came easily to her, even in the places where her handwriting had become illegible in her haste to write down all of her ideas. Cora glanced up at him and was surprised to see that his face did not betray the signs of confusion she had expected to see, but those of recognition.

"It's you..."

"What's me?" she replied, looking down at her arm again. "What do you mean?"

"You have to come with me," Alexander said in a sharp undertone, casting an uneasy glance at the other guards around him. It seemed that they were too far away from the entrance to attract any active attention from the knights on patrol. They would not get involved in a petty scuffle during their shift unless it was truly necessary.

"I'm not going anywhere with you! You wanted to take me to the *dungeons*!" Cora hissed.

"No, I didn't-"

"Yes, you did," she retorted. "I *know* you, Orion, I wrote you – wrote all of this!"

Alexander stood looking uncertain for a moment.

"Yes, yes you did," he said, his voice almost resigned. "This is why you know that you do not belong here with us."

"I guess, but that's in the nature of a dream, you know, temporary misplacement," she said with a shrug, before pulling her sleeves down to cover the writing. His expression turned into one of pity.

"You think this is a dream? Miss Sands, it is a far more serious situation..."

"Well of course you'd say that," Cora began, but he interrupted.

"We need to get you back to your world as soon as possible. Your presence makes the balance between the realms unstable and dangerous. The sooner you can get back to putting this world together from your side, the better – and, most importantly, before anyone else finds out that you're here," he said quietly. She stared at him, digesting this information.

"I'm sorry, but *what*?"

His grave and confidential manner suddenly evaporated and was replaced with the exasperated scowl she had written on his face more times than she cared to remember. Alexander's sharp nature had always been a burden for him. Now that he was faced with a dazed and confused seventeen year old girl, it seemed that he was already reaching the end of his limited patience.

"You know, considering your nature as the mother of all, you're not as intelligent as I had imagined you would be," he replied, a scathing note biting into his voice.

"It's not my fault if you have unnaturally high expectations of people," Cora said coolly. He raised his eyebrow at her, as if to say: *Yes it is.* Just then they were approached by one of the knights that had been standing in front of the city gates. He was a burly figure with dark features and an intimidating aura that fell around them with his shadow.

"Is there a problem, Orion?"

"Not at all, sir," Alexander replied swiftly. He stood carefully between them and she was rather under the impression that he was trying to shield her from the knight's curious gaze. "I was just about to show the new librarian's apprentice to her quarters."

"But the scuffle earlier…"

"A misunderstanding," he assured him. "She was a little overwhelmed when she came to the gates and it was difficult to understand her reasons for being here."

"I see…" the knight replied slowly, and for a moment Cora was certain that he did not believe Alexander's explanation. He then turned away from them and made his way back to the gates. "I will open the gates for you. Welcome to the city, apprentice."

"T-thank you," she replied hesitantly as Alexander half-pushed her through the gates in order to get out of the guard's line of view.

The buildings around them were made of deep blue marble, a material native to the surrounding area which gave the city its name. In contrast to the dark stone, the patches of white seemed to glow in the afternoon sunshine. Cora ran her hand unconsciously along the walls as she followed Alexander further into town. Imprints of words bloomed on the stone where she touched it, similar to those the knight had left on her own skin. Some of the townspeople stared after her. She was too distracted by her surroundings to pay them any attention. As Alexander led her into the inner-city, Cora began to recognise more locations from her writing; the fountain where the main character was introduced, the cliff-hanger ending to a chapter set on the main street and a bakery that would prove to be more important than any of the characters realised.

"Don't lag behind," Alexander called over his shoulder. A look of alarm flashed across his face when he saw what Cora had left on the walls behind her and he pulled her roughly away from them. "And stop doing that. Do you want someone to see you?"

"I suppose not," she replied, only half-paying attention to him. It was an incredible feeling to see and hear a world you created functioning around you. Suddenly everything that had existed only within her mind was only an arm's length away. She could even smell food she had never experienced, wafting down the street towards them.

"Cora," he snapped, shaking her by the arm. She blinked slowly and looked round at him, breaking out from her reverie.

"You called me Cora," she said as she pulled herself free from his grasp. "You never call people by their first name, even after their insistence. You say it keeps you professional."

He stared at her, confused and momentarily taken aback.

"I suppose having you here leaves more room for character development," Alexander replied. "My habits aren't so strictly bound when you're here and able to change them without much thought..."

"What is that supposed to mean?" Cora said as she followed him further down the main street towards the castle. There was a long pause where he did not reply.

"It means that it must be very easy for you to write tragic events when you don't have to experience them yourself," he said darkly. "I'm sure tragic characters must be very popular where you're from, as I cannot see any other reason why you would write such events into my past."

Cold realisation washed over her.

"Leona..."

Alexander glared over his shoulder at her, but said nothing.

"I'm so sorry," she said quietly. And she was; writing was something that she did for herself and it had never occurred to her that it might have an impact on someone else. Why would it have? Some writers dreamed of meeting their characters and yet she was sure that none of them had done so in such bizarre circumstances. "I didn't think... It was just a backstory. I needed a reason for you to want to become a knight."

He remained silent.

"I could rewrite it," Cora suggested. "Bring her back. I can fix it..."

"What's done is done," Alexander said coldly, his attention fixed on the road ahead.

"Well that's the thing about stories... they can be rewritten," she explained.

"Come on, we're nearly there," he sighed, ignoring her comment. Cora did not dare push the matter or ask where they were going. The reality was that there was little to harm her in a city that she had created, but it was better to go with the grain of events than fight against them. She had left too many plot holes to be certain that there was not something dark lurking in the shadows. For now, she would place her trust in familiarity and the strength of her main characters to get her home, however farfetched the idea actually was.

They had reached the inner-circle of the city; the district of pomp and riches that surrounded the castle. Here, the streets took on a different atmosphere. Silverwork decorated the buildings in an intricate web of patterns. There was less bustle and noise. People would nod to them as they passed. Cora assumed that this polite behaviour was directed at Alexander, with the royal crest of knighthood blazoned on his jacket sleeve and chest. Later she noticed that other passersby greeted each other in the same manner. Cora was more careful to keep in step with him now, keen to avoid being brought into conversation. It had been a sheer luck that Alexander had recognised her for what she was. It was likely that next time nothing would save her from her own tongue-tied lies.

The palace suddenly came into view, as though it had grown out of the buildings ahead. It was a beautiful, pale grey stone structure with tall turrets that jutted out like rays of light. It was the star at the heart of the city. Cora had little time to marvel at it as the knight pushed her on through the streets. She tried to catch glimpses of the castle face through the gaps between buildings. It had been the most difficult aspect of the city for her to imagine and now it was a few hundred metres away from her, its structure apparently defying gravity in the way the towers balanced at awkward angles away from the core. Alexander had taken her by the sleeve again and was half-dragging her in the right direction through the densely packed buildings.

"Here we are," he said finally, coming to a halt in front of a smaller door in the side of the palace wall. Cora recognised it as the door that the princess used to leave the castle unnoticed. Sunlight struggled to hit this corner of the building, making the stone seem a dirtier grey than it actually was, particularly in contrast to the glittering nature of the building she had seen as they approached.

The passage inside was cool and shady. They followed the stairs into the heart of the building, often turning so sharply that Cora forgot towards which part of the building they were now heading. Neither of them spoke. She had nothing to say and judging by the continued tense nature of his expression, Alexander was still upset after their last conversation. He mutely unlatched the door they had stopped in front of and let it swing open onto a brightly lit corridor.

It was a tall, arched space with sharp stone carvings set into the walls on either side. It was the corridor that held the palace library and the home of Lady Jenna Hastings, the royal book keeper and literary scholar. With some effort, Alexander pushed the thick oak doors of the library open. They grumbled in protest as the wood dragged across the stone floor. Cora followed him inside.

"What have I told you about barging in here, unannounced?" Jenna called from the top of a bookshelf to their right. She slid down the ladder easily, landing with a light thud before marching over to them. Alexander turned to close the doors behind him.

"Show her your arm, Miss Sands," he said, unperturbed by the librarian's aggression.

"What's going on?" Jenna asked. She seemed less irritated now that he had closed the doors behind them. Many of the knights had a reputation for having little respect for her work and out of habit she resented them. Cora pulled up her sleeve.

"I'm-" she began, but Jenna cut across her.

"I know who you are," she said quietly. She held Cora's arm up for inspection without asking for permission, a small frown creasing her dark features. Her eyes flicked over to where Alexander was standing as she read the markings. "I had hoped that I would never see this."

As Cora let her arm fall to her side, she noticed that new words had appeared where Jenna had been holding her hand and briefly wondered how many more encounters she would have to endure before her whole arm was covered in character notes.

"See what? The writing?" she asked, rubbing at her hand subconsciously.

"That's not writing," Jenna explained. "Well, technically it is, but really it's a mark of the imbalance between the two worlds. The bridge between us and you has been broken. If you're on this side of the story, who is out there to write the rest of it?"

"The rest of it?" Cora repeated, confused. "What rest of it? I stopped writing years ago."

"Just because you've stopped writing doesn't mean that the story stops living, Cora," she said patiently. "We live in you."

"Clearly, as I'm the only person mad enough to dream up this scenario!"

Jenna and Alexander exchanged a look.

"She thinks this is a dream," he said calmly, as he leaned against the nearest table. "I thought I had managed to convince her otherwise, but she keeps falling back into old convictions."

Jenna sighed.

"It is very possible that she's asleep," she admitted. "Few states of being thin the barrier enough to allow someone to cross into this realm… but this isn't a dream. Dreaming is a temporary, fragile state. Our world of imagination has no such time limit; we exist alongside their world. You can't have one without the other. We need to get her back home as quickly as possible, before things begin to escalate. She can only be here for so long without serious repercussions – ones I can't even bear thinking about…"

Cora stared at the pair of them, not sure what to think. It all seemed somehow too complicated and yet obvious now that Jenna had provided an explanation. There was no reason why reality and imagination could not exist in balance together.

"Then get me home," Cora said finally, letting herself believe the impossible. "Tell me what needs doing; what will it take to get -"

The library doors swung open with a loud bang, causing them all jump. It seemed that the wood protested less under the great force of multiple palace guards.

"Your majesty," Jenna and Alexander said in unison, as they fell into a deep bow for the arrival of the king. The librarian tugged on Cora's pushed up sleeve and pulled the writer to her knees beside them. The king gestured his approval as he entered the room. Although they all stood up, Jenna kept her hand over the cloth on Cora's wrist.

"Lady Hastings, I have been informed that an important guest was seen making their way to your quarters and I insisted on making my way over here to greet them myself," the king said, his blue eyes fixed on Cora. Unable to hold his piercing gaze, she looked away.

"A guest, your majesty?" Jenna replied, her tone one of polite confusion. "There is no-one here but Sir Orion and my... assistant."

A slight frown passed across the king's face. He was a tall, thin man with greying hair and sharp features. Cora knew him to be impatient and stubborn. He stepped further into the room.

"Your assistant?" King Leones. "Pray tell, what use does a librarian have for an assistant?"

This time, Jenna did not miss a beat.

"Your collection has been growing for many years, your majesty, and I'm afraid that I felt the need to take on another pair of hands in order to keep organisation to the standard you require," she explained calmly. His lip twitched.

"And you did not think to consult me on such matters?" he demanded. "You should have thought to consult me before bringing any old soul off the streets and into the castle."

"You are right, your majesty. I should have consulted you, but at the time I did not want to bother you with such trivial matters. It is not your responsibility to look after the castle staff, after all," she replied lightly, careful not to run him into an argument.

"Be that as it may, I feel it is my responsibility to welcome her to our palace family personally..." he continued and the librarian suddenly looked wary.

"That is very kind of you, your majesty, but we really have a lot to get through before dinner. I'm sure she will be happy to join you tomorrow morning, as soon as you see fit to call upon her," Jenna insisted. Cora stood very still, her gaze flicking between them, feeling anxious. She could not understand why the king was paying such attention to her. It seemed almost out of character.

"In that case, she must have dinner with me," he replied brightly, before turning to the guard nearest to him. "In fact, we will have it right now. Alert the kitchen!"

Cora felt, rather than saw Jenna stiffen beside her, and she knew that whatever mute plan that had existed between her and Alexander had failed. The king's word was final. Cora had no choice but to leave them and follow him from the library.

"I have to apologise for my staff," said the king, as the guards pulled the library doors closed behind them. "Clearly they are not as... well acquainted with your abilities as I am."

"What abilities?" Cora asked, as they began to make their way up the corridor in the opposite direction from the one she had taken less than an hour ago.

"Come now, there's no need to be so reserved about the matter," he laughed. "I have eyewitnesses from the lower city who can testify to your powers. What you can do with just a wave of your hand is nothing compared to what you can do when you put your mind to it, I'm sure..."

"I really don't know what you're talking about," she replied apologetically. The king stopped walking and in one swift movement he pulled her wrist up to eye level to reveal the markings. She met his cold gaze for a second before pulling her hand out of his grasp. "You think a few words on my wrist mean that I have some sort of magical power?"

"They are an indication," he nodded. "But the truth is that we have been expecting you..."

"How could you have been expecting me?" Cora demanded, dropping all pretence of ignorance. "I wrote nothing about myself in this story."

"Every author leaves their mark on their own handiwork," he replied. "And it just so happens that we found yours..."

They had reached another set of doors, this time smaller than those of the library. Two of the guards rushed forward to open them. Beyond the doors was a room; not small, but not large compared to most of the other rooms in the palace. It was clear that a great deal had been done to ensure the upkeep of the room. Everything was impeccably clean and the seating around them appeared never to have been used. The room was made up of pale stone walls, but Cora could see no windows. Curtains appeared to serve only as decoration. The king led her to the centre of the room and gestured to the tall pedestal in front of them.

On the pedestal sat an hourglass. It was only about the size of the palm of her hand and had a silver chain wrapped around its centre so that it could be worn as a necklace. The king reached out a hand and picked it up to show it to her.

"Its meaning must seem obvious to you, now that you have seen it," he said, letting it hang from his fingertips. Cora noticed that the sand did not pass from one chamber to the other. "Cora Sands leaves us a broken hourglass..."

She said nothing as she stared at it, wracking her brain to work out why her subconscious would chose to leave an hourglass as a mark in her fantasy world. It could be a simple play on her surname, but there was something about the way it was hanging, perfectly balanced in front of her, that suggested otherwise.

"I know you have the ability to create anything. I mean, we exist because of you! I would like you to work for me. The conditions are very reasonable, mark you; food, clothing, anything else you could possibly want, but most of all... your safety. There's only so much of this place you can know, after all..." the king said quietly, as he returned the glass to the iron pedestal.

"Are you threatening me?" Cora asked warily.

He laughed.

"You misunderstand me..."

"No, you misunderstand me," she insisted. "You know that this entire city cannot exist unless I am at home to write it, don't you?"

"Of course, but that is a temporary boundary – it can be rewritten," he smiled. "Think of the team we would make. Imagine, living in your dream world forever... Would it not be the greatest opportunity for you?"

Cora hesitated. In life, there were many things that did not suit her. Everybody had their bad days; at work, at school, at home. There were things that she wished she could change, both personal and universal, but could she give it all away to live in a world where she dictated everything around her? No; it would be overwhelming and more pressure than she could imagine. Life existed as a complex mixture of good and bad, but in the end bad moments passed and unexpected surprises could become glorious memories that you cherished forever.

Forever...

Forever was an awfully long time. She would miss life at home. It would be so lonely to live in a world where you could ensure that everybody treated you well. They would not be real relationships. Even if she did decide to recreate people from home, they would merely be shadows of themselves. She would never be able to shake the consciousness of them being something that she had simply written. There was no guarantee that she even *could* create characters now that she was in the city. While it had been interesting to face her characters for a little while, Cora was certain that to spend all of her time with them would be too much.

She had to go home. Fantasy was a break from everyday life, but to let it become her entire world was out of the question. In the same way that the story lives on after the book is closed, Cora had to return so that she could live her own story - life.

"No," she said sharply.

"I beg your pardon?"

"I said, no. I reject your offer," Cora replied, her voice stronger now. "I'm going home."

A dark shadow fell across the king's face.

"I'm sure we could change your mind..." he said, the muscles tightening slightly in his jaw. He was used to getting everything he wanted, but not this time.

"You can't. It is my final answer," she retorted. They stood glaring at each other; all pretence of affability was gone. Cora now remembered his power-hungry nature and the problems it caused. There was a reason why the people of the Star City were waiting for his daughter to take the throne.

"Very well... *Guards!*"

The doors swung open to reveal a mass of people standing in the corridor, each dressed in deep blue uniforms. The king left, his deep blue cloak billowing out behind him as he stalked away. In a few seconds, the doors had been slammed shut behind him and Cora was left staring at the minuscule gap between the panels of wood. She thumped the door loudly with her fist, yelling for them to let her go, but nobody replied.

"Typical," she sighed, letting herself slump forward and pressing her forehead against the dark oak. There was no way that she would be able to escape via the corridor ahead. There were too many people outside and it was too conspicuous to leave by the main entrance. There had to be some way to get back to Jenna and Alexander. She turned slowly to examine the room.

Other than the set of armchairs and sofas in the middle of the room, the space was sparsely furnished. A pair of curtains hung from the far wall in order to create the impression of windows. It was clear that this room was nothing more than a comfortable prison. There was a bookshelf in one corner and a desk in the other. It did not take long for Cora to inspect every inch of the room. It was clear that the two doors were the only exit.

She found herself standing in front of the pedestal, staring down at the hourglass. It seemed strange to think that this unimpressive object was the piece of herself she had left behind. She reached out and picked it up. It was lighter than it looked. Cora twirled it absently on its chain. It was only when it had stopped that she realised something; the sand had started to run. The hourglass was not broken at all. It was as though it had been waiting for her touch all along.

A long moment passed as she watched the sand run into the other chamber. Cora then flipped it over in her hand to return the grains to sand to their original space; but the direction the sand was moving in did not change. Even upside down, the sand ran into the empty chamber. A dull feeling of dread had settled in the pit of her stomach. There was only one thing that the glass could be counting towards in response to her touch. She had to get out of the room and back to the library as quickly as possible. Jenna was the only person who could tell her how to get home.

Cora raced around the room once more, looking for anything that could help her escape. She let books fall to the ground and left no space unchecked; she even pulled up the rug in the middle of the room, just in case there was a trapdoor hidden beneath. The curtains fell to the floor in a great *whoosh* of fabric as they came free from their rings. Blank stone walls stared at her on all sides. The desk drawers rattled as she opened them, but there was nothing inside except a few scraps of paper and a broken pen.

There was nothing inside except a few scraps of paper and a broken pen.

Cora pulled them frantically out of the drawer, praying that the crack in the pen was only a surface wound. *A wave of your hand... put your mind to it...* The king's words echoed in her mind as she scribbled in the corner of one of the sheets of paper. Ink flourished on the page and although it was splotchy in parts, the pen seemed to be working. *Put your mind to it...* If she could reverse her writing technique just by touching something, perhaps writing something here would bring it to life. She stared at the page. Her heart was racing, but for a moment her mind had gone blank. She had to start small; there was no point getting overexcited about an idea she could not use. Cora ran her tongue over her teeth, vaguely aware that she was thirsty.

Cora was thirsty. She paused. *Suddenly, a glass of water appeared on the desk beside her.*

There was a long moment where Cora did nothing but stare intently at the desk in front of her, wishing for the writing to work. Nothing happened. She sighed, running a hand through her dark hair and looking gloomily around the rest of the room in the hope that the instructions had been followed inaccurately. It appeared they had not. She turned her attention abruptly back to the desk, moving so quickly that she knocked the newly created glass of water flying across the table. Cora let out a great "*Ha!*" of triumph and let a grin spread across her face. It had worked. After all of the king's speech about using her powers, she would now be able to use them against him.

She found herself staring at the scrap of yellowing paper once again.

"What do I write next?" she muttered. "Where do I even start?"

It had been a problem at home and it appeared to still be a problem now; after all of her work on planning the story and developing the characters, Cora found that the most difficult thing in writing was putting the first few sentences down on paper. Once she had begun to write, things became much easier. She could spend metaphorical eons staring at a blank page, but not this time.

Behind the bookcase stood a long corridor that led into the depths of the castle. Cora approached it nervously. As she stepped inside, the torches burst into a path of gentle candlelight. The corridor led her straight into the library, where she found Jenna and Alexander waiting for her in the armchairs in the middle of the room.

Cora glanced over the writing in front of her before stuffing the paper and pen into her pockets and racing towards the bookshelf. She could only hope that the glass of water had not been a coincidence. With a great deal of effort, the bookcase slid along the wall to reveal a shadowy passageway. As she stepped inside, the candles burst violently into light and Cora had to duck to the ground to avoid being scorched.

"I should probably have been less dramatic in my description..." she said, straightening once again as the candles died down and became nothing more than gentle lamplight.

Unable to stop herself, Cora raced down the corridor, the hourglass bumping against her stomach with every step. It was smaller than a real hourglass; therefore it was difficult to tell how much time she really had. Footsteps echoed along the narrow space. Her feet seemed to be running without her now. She had the strangest feeling that she would topple over if she tried to make any sudden breaks in her sprint.

Just then, the door at the end of the corridor began to come into view, less than fifty metres away. It was difficult to slow down now that she had become accustomed to the rush of movement. In the end, Cora managed to hit the door with a gentle *thud* before she pushed it open and entered the library, gasping for air.

"Cora!" Jenna cried, sounding both relieved and impressed as she ran over to her. Alexander followed quickly after her, his sword clattering against the bookshelves in his haste to reach them.

"How did you get here?" he asked as they helped bring her into the centre of the room. Cora pulled the scraps of paper out of her pocket and shoved them at him in response as she tried to catch her breath. She could not remember the last time she had had to run like that in real life. Alexander mouthed the words as he read. "So that's why he wanted you…"

"I know, I know, I should have listened to you…" she sighed, kicking her legs out in front of her to rid them of the tingling feeling after her run. "Kept out of sight and all that…"

"Well yes," Alexander replied with a shrug. "But even I did not think the king would be the one to capture you. It seems… very unlike him."

"That's because you place too much faith in authority," Cora replied. "Jenna knew what was happening the minute the guards walked in… I could see it in her face."

Jenna said nothing to this, but was staring at the chain around Cora's neck.

"Is that what I think it is?" she asked curiously, reaching her hand out for it.

"It's my mark on this world," Cora explained as she handed it to her. "Cora Sands and the sands of time…"

"It's also running out," Jenna observed. "We need to get you out of here as quickly as we can, without drawing attention to ourselves."

"How are we going to do that?"

"We need to find the thinnest point between the Star City and your world. It will act as a gateway. Dreams are the thinnest point in reality, so what's the thinnest point in the story?" she asked, fixing her attention on the writer's face. Cora stared back at her.

"I don't know… the ending maybe?" she said hesitantly, uncertain now that she was placed under such pressure. In that moment, everything seemed to fall into place. It all seemed so obvious now; every part of the story had a reason. "The ending is the thinnest point because it's when the reader must leave the story and go back to their own life."

"So where does the story end?" Alexander asked.

"Right here."

Imaginings
Navleen Kalsi

"Why are you following me?" she asks, not really knowing what answer she is searching for. The air is heavy, she feels like she is swimming, drowning in the weight of it. His response floats towards her, she almost picks it up, finds his hand instead.

"To do this," a quick two-step that is dangerously close to the edge. Her body is pressed against his and their hands are clasped. Immediately her heart flutters but she cannot interpret it, her heart and head speak two different languages and she is not bilingual. She was completely unaware of an edge until he appeared and now she has to cling to him for her life. She does not know where she is, whether she is inside or out, all she knows is that if she were to fall now it would be a very long time before she hit the ground.

Awakening abruptly, the girl wonders if she will see him today. Perhaps this is the day.

The cold air wisps around her; she is cold. Four hours, three minutes and eleven seconds crawl past until she sees him again. Their eyes lock and she struggles to pull them away, desperately wanting to seem cool and aloof. He does not pursue her, he does not care.

A forest now. An idyllic setting for a fairy tale. One in which the beautiful girl waits for her handsome prince to return. She stands there waiting, the bare ground frozen beneath her. The ghostly, naked trees surrounding her. She is so alone, he does not come.

He ignores her the next day in the harsh reality of daylight. These mind games are tantalising, she feels like she has no control over her destiny when all she wants is to kiss him.

Now our protagonist is asleep. And since she knows she is asleep, it is her turn to take control. So she runs through her own imagination, bursting through various scenes she has collected from countless Hollywood films and her own adventures. Sunsets, snowstorms, glorious beaches are all dismissed in seconds. Opting instead for her childhood back garden, she sits upon a swing and waits. The one beside her is empty. She knows he will come for this is her fantasy; she decides. Finally. He arrives, dishevelled, sweating. Did he run here too? "I love you" she says, letting the words drop, sinking heavily to the ground. But he already knows this, he has known all along. Taking the seat in the swing beside her, the picture finally seems complete, and as he reaches to kiss her it seems like the most natural thing.

Smiling, she awakes. To her comfortless bed, squashed in between four grey walls. The sun glares through the unwashed windows as she realises it was a dream. Facing this day is much harder than the others.

Today he comes to her. She throws together some witty comments in her mind, ideas to sound funny and somewhat interesting to him. Sighing instead, about to explain that she loves him and has no reason why. He laughs and he smiles. "I know, I was there."

Polygamy and Other Metaphysical Problems
Hussain Ajina

1

Stephen ran across the street to his car, bent over double in a vain attempt to avoid the hammering rain. As he reached it he opened the door, slipped into his seat, closed the door behind him and slid the key into the ignition, all in a single, fluid motion. He turned the key and the engine roared into life. Grasping the steering wheel he flicked his lights on, watching with a faint feeling of satisfaction as they flared up at the front, bouncing reflections off deep puddles in the road. He made to move off, taking one last glance at the building he'd just left. He could see the window of her flat, still slightly open, the curtain fluttering furiously in the wind. She was nowhere to be seen. She.

He'd called her "she" years ago, when he'd first known her. Not in speech, since he'd never spoken to anyone about her, but even in his own head it had hurt to think of her name. He could think it now of course: Lucy, and say it too, if need be, but all those years ago things seemed very different. Wanting her, desiring her, seeing in her the epitome of beauty, perfected in every way, and not being able to be with her, it had hurt him more than he cared to admit. He'd told no one- an inability to explain the inexplicable, combined with a fear of outright derision had kept his lips shut- yet all the while a wild fire blazed within, burning up his insides. And he'd called her "she". The more he'd thought about her, the more he'd perfected her, immortalising her, making her in his mind so much more than she'd ever been in reality. Time passed and life went on, and as Stephen moved on with his life she slipped quietly to the back of his mind. He never forgot her, though; she remained there, glowing like a star, a tiny pinprick of light burning away in the darkness, somewhere deep within him.

Then, years later, she had suddenly reappeared, beautiful as ever and gloriously human, and all at once everything became so easy. He simply stretched out his hand and, barely thinking, lazily even, he took her, and just like that she fell into place beside him, as comfortably and naturally as Stephen slid into his car seat. And now he called her "Lucy"; but old habits died hard.

The rainwater slid across the windscreen, coming down almost faster than the window-wipers could wipe it away. All the lights of the night- from car headlamps, traffic lights, streetlamps- came streaming through the windows, refracted and strangely blurred by the water. The reflections passed over the interior of the car as it moved through the night, over the seats and the dashboard, and over Stephen's pensive features. He felt dirty, snake-like, slithering back home. Aglaya would be waiting for him, suspecting maybe; he'd stayed at Lucy's longer than he'd intended to, longer than was prudent, longer than was really necessary. The thought of Aglaya waiting almost broke his heart. He could picture her now, his wife, standing by the window in the semi-darkness, not having bothered to draw the curtains or turn on the lights, absent-mindedly watching the street, streams of rain sliding into the gutters, wondering where he was. Why did he deceive her? Was it worth it? The simple answer was he didn't know. He loved Aglaya, he knew that much. She was warmth, sustaining him, constantly giving him life. Sometimes, when he lay next to her at night, he could feel her body exuding heat. Gently, he would place his hand on her bare arm and feel her blood pulsing beneath her skin. It felt so warm and alive and, when he drew back his hand, he could almost imagine, in the darkness, that he'd left a glowing palm-print on her arm. The thought of being without her was unendurable for Stephen; even now, as the thought flitted through his mind, it seemed to tug down at his insides, trying to pull him beneath the earth. But then there was Lucy? Lucy...

Lucy, Lucy, light of my life.

The words came unbidden to his mind, carved into his brain through years of constant yearning, and as immovable as the sun and all the stars. He loved Lucy, he loved Aglaya. He knew it was wrong, but he knew nothing more.

The various cars on the road sent spray shooting from their rear-tyres, flying up behind them, illuminated red in mid-air by tail and brake lights. Every now and again, it seemed that blue lights flashed out before his eyes. They flashed elusive, fleetingly, his eyes flicking about, trying to focus on them, and every time the lights would slide sideways, suddenly no longer where they were. They weren't really there- they were products of his mind, sensory reactions to his thoughts and feelings, synaesthesia the doctor had called it, or something like that- but he tried to follow them nonetheless. They put him in mind of police-car lights. The thought made him anxious and he glanced in the rear-view mirror. No police there, only car headlamps, shining through the rain.

All the various lights, real and imagined, the blues, the reds and the oranges, streamed through the windows and the rain. They coalesced on Stephen's eyes, ending up as a single, indistinct blur. The whole world became a vague haze.

2

The car ground to a stop by the sodden curb. Stephen left his car absent-mindedly, pausing to take a deep breath of the fresh night air. The rain had stopped and the aftermath of the storm seemed to be a muffling blanket, covering everything with stillness and silence. He trod furtively up to the front door and slowly slipped his key into the lock. It turned with a satisfying clunk and the door slid open. Stephen entered, letting the door close behind him. It was quite dark within; as he'd imagined, Aglaya hadn't bothered to light up when the sun had set, and eerie orange streetlamp light streamed blurrily passed the undrawn curtains. She wasn't standing by the window, however, and the faint glow of a table-lamp told him she was in the living room. Sure enough, he found her there, curled up in a chair, both legs swept away to the side, reading a book in the dim light.

"Hello," said Stephen cautiously. She didn't turn from her book.

"There's a letter for you," she said, gesturing towards the table in front of her where a manila envelope casually lay. Her words had the faint trace of a Slavic accent, though her jet-black hair betrayed her Romani roots. Stephen moved forward to take the letter but at the same moment Aglaya reached out and picked it up. She looked up and offered it to him. Stephen looked right into her eyes, her bright brown Gypsy eyes, and felt a hook pull down at his insides. *She suspected.* All Stephen's guilt and self-loathing blossomed up inside him and he felt that he couldn't deceive her any longer. He would look straight into her eyes and tell her everything, about Lucy and… But then Lucy would be…

He looked down at the letter and read his name and address on the envelope. He recognised the handwriting, but it wasn't *hers*. He hurriedly snatched the letter from Aglaya's hand and stuffed it into his inside jacket pocket, careless of how it creased under his rough touch. He made to turn away.

"Well," said Aglaya, "who's it from?" Stephen didn't stop and made slowly for the stairs.

"I don't know yet," he said simply.

"Aren't you going to open it?"

"Later."

Though his back was turned to her, Stephen could feel Aglaya's fierce glare burning into his back and at that moment he felt more like a wretched snake then ever. He couldn't bear to turn around, to meet her eyes once more. He just felt, with all his soul, that he needed to get away, to be alone for a while. He slithered up the stairs and made his way to his study. Flicking on the light switch, he shut the study door firmly behind him and drew the curtains. The light flickered on and off, occasionally plunging the room into pitch darkness for a few seconds before sputtering back into life. There must have been something wrong with the bulb.

Leaning against the closed door, Stephen slid down to sit on the floor and pulled the crumpled letter from his pocket. He didn't know why he'd refused to tell Aglaya who had sent it. He had known, the second he saw those slanting letters spelling out his name, but he'd pretended he hadn't. "I don't know," he'd said; a barefaced lie, right there. And so pointless. He hadn't hidden anything incriminating, there was no reason Aglaya *shouldn't* know who'd sent it. She might even find out, eventually. But the lie slid out of his mouth as smoothly and naturally as his key into the lock. The psychologist inside him told him that this was a natural consequence of his deceitful lifestyle, that he'd become so used to lying in order to protect the intricate web of deceit that he'd built around himself that he was now unable to stop himself. But Stephen felt something deeper, a fundamental instinct to be private, to be the sole owner of his own thoughts. That's why he'd come to this room, why he was leaning against the door; to read the letter without the destabilising presence of others. The light flickered furiously above.

Stephen slid his finger beneath the envelope's seal and tore it open in one, swift movement. He took out the handwritten sheets of paper that emerged and began to read.

Stephen!

How long has it been? Honestly, I daren't count the years since last we met. Since then the earth has turbulated on, spinning round and round the fiery sun more times than I care to remember. It's a wonder we're all not staggering dizzily around, clinging on to chairs and leaning on walls. And in all that time, what could have happened? Lives continue to be lived, regardless of our wishes. Everything continues to change, people grow older, spawn and then shuffle off into their mortal graves. Perhaps this has happened to you, though I sincerely hope it hasn't. Perhaps I'm writing to a dead man. In any regard, there is one piece of solid information we can salvage from all this uncertainty and confusion. It has been too *long.*

The last time we were together I told you that I intended to go on a long journey, to get away from the tedious inevitability of our city lives. You know very well how much that irked me, and how desperately I yearned to flee from it all, to, once and for all, escape. Let me tell you now how futile my attempt was. I moved from place to place, from meal to meal, scraping a living any way I could. I pursued the nomadic life in aspiration of my Bedouin forefathers, but all the while the necessity to eat and drink, and have somewhere sheltered to sleep, and the necessity to earn money to achieve all this, pulled me incessantly to the urban superglotts. I eventually found- I won't tell where or for how long- that I'd become a thoroughly sedentary individual, and that I'd been caught up in the web of modern domestic mediocrity that I'd so prided myself in rejecting. At that moment I set my heart on escape. Long, dark nights I plotted, calculating distances and travel expenses, living costs, wages and thirty-days notice. And then, when the moment arrived, I grasped it with both hands and set out on my final journey: homewards.

I'm writing this letter in a God-forsaken little shack that they insist on calling a hotel room, and I should be back home within the week. I emerge from my perilous journey battered, bruised, in possession of a little more knowledge perhaps, or maybe some world-weariness, but ultimately, gloriously, completely and joyously alive! And so, of course, this is what this has all been about, we must meet again. I shall come to visit you exactly two week from the date of this letter. You haven't really any say in the matter, but I thought I'd let you know as a matter of common courtesy. I'm sure you're looking forward to our reunion. I am.

> *You are forever,*
> *My love my hope and all my dreams,*
> *Yours and all that,*
> *Dhiyaa.*

Stephen smiled to himself. Dhiyaa... it *had* been a long time since Stephen had seen him last, but it seemed that the years hadn't changed him. He was still the same, overly dramatic, ridiculously verbose man he was all those years ago. Even at school, where Stephen and Dhiyaa had first known each other, he was constantly waving his hands around expressively, expounding upon this or that idea. So, Dhiyaa was coming back then? It would be good to see those dramatic hand gestures again.

The light-bulb blinked. It had been flickering all the while Stephen was reading Dhiyaa's letter, the periods of darkness becoming longer and longer as it went on. And now it blinked and faded to black, and it was a good eight seconds before it burst back into light. Stephen heard, away on the other side of the house, Aglaya mounting the stairs, making her way to bed. He'd tell her about Dhiyaa and his letter tomorrow. He smiled to himself again; he'd missed his friend more than he'd realised, and it really would be good to see him again. The bulb shimmered gently, winking once, twice, thrice... then, with the quietest of tinks, the filament came apart, falling into the bulb's base. The room fell into utter darkness.

3

"Hmm..." Dhiyaa gave a rumble of consideration as he took in everything Stephen had told him. "It seems to me that you're in a right quandary and no mistake."

The two of them were in Stephen's car, Stephen driving, Dhiyaa reclining in the passenger seat, both moving slowly through traffic in Hyde Park. It was very hot and the windows were open, the sun was blazing down upon them from a cloudless sky. Everything seemed so vivid in the brilliant, white sunlight. The green of the grass and the reds, blues and purples from the flowerbeds seemed to leap up towards them, clawing at the edges of the windows, trying to get in. Stephen had just been filling his friend in on his problem with Lucy and Aglaya, and Dhiyaa's response was less than he'd hoped for.

"Do you think I'm horrible?" Stephen asked.

"Not at all," said Dhiyaa, "it seems to me you're as much a victim here as anyone else."

"A victim? Don't you understand? I'm the duplicitous one here. I'm the bastard hiding in the shadows, cheating, ceaselessly desiring women-"

"I understand perfectly," Dhiyaa interjected, "the problem here, the real, the one at the *bottom* of all this, isn't *your* polygamy, but the polygamous instinct in general, if that even really *is* a problem." Stephen's eyes narrowed beneath the sweltering heat.

"Explain," he said, shortly. Dhiyaa fancied himself something of a great thinker, Stephen knew that, and though his ideas were often fanciful and needlessly elaborate, they were seldom without any substance. A slight smile stole over Dhiyaa's face before he began his exposition.

"Well, I suppose what it all *really* comes down," he said, "is the blind acceptance of what we're told is right and wrong when it comes to the question of sexuality. You see, you and I, and pretty much everyone else in the world, have been brought up to believe that there's a particular attitude towards sex and love that's standard and correct. The demonisation of polygamy, the compartmentalisation of mental and physical existence, that is to say, setting 'looks' against 'personality', even the general condemnation of, as you put it, 'ceaselessly desiring women'. All this we accept by rote, not taking a moment to question such attitudes, to think about their validity. But, if you stop for a second, look deep within *yourself*, if you take your cues from how *you* feel, rather than how society tells you you *should* feel, a different picture emerges, doesn't it? I know, the polygamous impetus, it lies deep inside your chest, as it does in mine, and every other man in the world, constantly pushing us further. Are we then evil, simply being as we *are*? To constantly desire women, isn't that really what it means to be a man?" Dhiyaa was becoming more and more animated as he spoke, and with those last words he swirled his finger in a dramatic, horizontal circle, like an ancient Roman orator. Stephen glanced over at him, sceptically.

"You're not convinced, I see," Dhiyaa continued. "Well, think of this then. Have you ever asked yourself why you began your affair with Lucy to begin with? Wasn't Aglaya good enough for you? Weren't you *satisfied*? The dominant social attitude will levy these accusatory questions at you, but they fail to acknowledge the truth. There *is* no satisfaction. When it comes to the male sexual desire, the question of satisfaction simply doesn't exist. There is no such thing as enough. The male sexual desire is completely insatiable.

"Do you need proof? Look within yourself, that's where the *real* proof lies. You can feel it, the endless desire pulsing in your temples, the perpetually repeated command: 'More, more, more!' Never satisfied, never quashed, the desire boils away in your blood. You can feel it, the latent energy swirling around in your pelvis, the single, basic instinct coded into every cell in your body, burning in your brain, to *thrust!*"

Stephen gently pressed down on the brakes as they approached a zebra crossing. A young woman stood on the pavement, waiting for his car to stop. Her bare shoulders glistened in the summer sun. The makeup she wore was plain to see, an attempt to smooth away the face, to pursue an ideal beauty, but in the intense sunlight Stephen could almost see through her makeup, right down to the rose red grain of her skin. And he *could* feel it, his breath catching in his lungs and, deep in his pelvic bones, the energy pulling him forward, urging him to...

The woman reached the other side of the road and Stephen moved off again, passing over the zebra crossing. The sun blared through the windscreen, right into his eyes. He let his breath fall out of his nostrils. Dhiyaa was looking at him, a small smile of victory on his face.

"See," he said, "you can feel it."

"But this is different," said Stephen, "I'm talking about love, Dhiyaa, not just random instances of sexual attraction. Aglaya, Lucy, I *love* them both, and I can't find any way of resolving that."

"Why do you love them?" asked Dhiyaa.

"I- what?" Stephen hadn't been expecting this question and it'd caught him off guard.

"I said: why do you love them?"

"What do you mean, 'why'?"

"What, for instance, do you love about them?"

"I..." Stephen began, expecting the answer to flow out easily of its own accord, but it wasn't forthcoming and his voice trailed away. What *did* he love about them?

He had *learned* to love Aglaya, he knew that much; or maybe 'learned' wasn't quite right. Compelled to love her, maybe, his affections unwittingly captured like a wild pokémon. She had been there first, loving him before he'd ever loved her, and slowly his heart opened up to her, letting her slightly further and further in. She gave him love and exacted a like gift in return, a gift Stephen hadn't realised he'd given until long after the giving. Not that he resented her for it; his love was no less genuine for having been cultivated. He could feel it now, as he could whenever he thought about Aglaya, warmth gently pulsing in his chest. But nevertheless, he knew he'd never *chosen* to love Aglaya. It had simply happened, creeping around him like an amorous ivy, and now he was so deeply ensnared he couldn't imagine life without.

Lucy was a different story. He cast his thoughts back, trying to recreate in his mind the first time he'd seen Lucy. It was that experience that had converted him to the idea of 'love at first sight'. She sat, untroubled, on a deep windowsill, her legs dangling carelessly over the edge and soft sunlight streaming in from the window behind her. He'd looked up into her face and she'd looked down into his, their eyes locked and they just stayed there for a moment, looking at each other, wordless. Stephen had never known for how long that moment lasted; it had seemed like the whole world was standing still, giving the two of them all the time they needed to look at each other, motionless. The sunlight danced in her hair, which fell freely over her shoulders, seeming to make it flutter as though in a light breeze. He could see life in her eyes, bursting out from the streaks of black in her irises. It was almost as though life was flowing down from where she sat, fluttering like veils in the wind, right into Stephen's heart. He could feel his pupils expanding, drinking in her sight. Every detail of her face became startlingly clear, as though illuminated by an intense light. And there, the rose red grain of her skin...

But there wasn't anything explicable, no particular thing that he could point at. There was no *why*. There was only the unquestionable fact that he loved them both. Dhiyaa simply sat there, looking at him, with the same, knowing smile.

"It's not different at all, is it?" he said. "People talk about love and people talk about lust, but don't they realise that they are one and the same thing, or at the very least that the one springs forth from the other? Love is in itself a form of sexual desire, a concentrated form perhaps. Doesn't it all, in the end, come down to the same sensations, the same instincts? To keep and to hold, to love and to thrust. And there is nothing at all indecent about love." Stephen scowled. He couldn't deny that there was truth in what

Dhiyaa was saying, and that he recognised himself in these descriptions.

"Are you saying," said Stephen, "that I'm morally justified to have affairs?"

"No, not really. Deception, I would say, is always bad, and you know that if your wife found out she'd be pretty hurt, and hurting others is pretty much the definition of immorality. However, I can't find it in my heart to blame you; I can only pity you."

Pity? Stephen's scowl deepened. Pity didn't help, it didn't solve any problems for him. The sun seemed to press down upon him with both its heat and its light. Stephen felt like he was suffocating in the brightness. The park was too vivid, too full of light. Sunlight was everywhere, all around him, and slowly he felt himself being consumed in the terrible, burning whiteness.

4

It was evening now and the sun was low in the sky. Stephen and Dhiyaa were walking along the river, west towards where the sun hung lazily over the horizon, the water lapping softly against the Strand. Stephen dragged his feet morosely across the sand. Thinking about both Aglaya and Lucy, and talking about them with Dhiyaa, had made him thoroughly embittered. He felt helpless, sorrow swelling in his chest. It was the same sorrow, he realised now, that he felt pulling down at his insides when he'd taken Dhiyaa's letter from Aglaya, looking down into her eyes. But now it was framed by a hateful knowing, a certainty that he was doomed to be forever torn between the two of them, Lucy and Aglaya, forever enmeshed in lies and deceit. He felt so terribly wretched, and the thought of being so for the rest of his life made him despair.

"How can I continue to *be* like this?" he burst out, suddenly animated.

"Are you so sure that you *are*, at all?"

"What?" asked Stephen, sharply.

"I was just wondering," Dhiyaa began in a slow, mischievous voice, "how you can be so certain of your own existence. It doesn't seem all that clear cut to me." Stephen gave him a long, sideways look of exasperation.

"Well," he said, sighing deeply, "didn't Descartes have something to say on the subject? Cogito ergo sum, and all that. If I'm aware of my own thoughts then it's fairly safe to assume that I do exist."

"I wonder about that..." Dhiyaa trailed off into silence, but Stephen didn't say anything. Dhiyaa took his silence as an invitation to embark upon another of his florid expositions.

"Think about this," he said. "What is it, really, that makes you you, as opposed to anyone else? What is it that determines the substance of those thoughts you're aware of, your own thoughts? I would say it's your memories and your experiences. The sum total of all the things you've thought and all the life you've lived, that all culminates to form your mind as it thinks and breathes. If you'd lived a different life, if you'd experienced different experiences and thought different thoughts, you'd undoubtedly be a different person. In short, you wouldn't be *you*.

"But now think of this. When you're asleep and when you dream, you're plunged into a different world, and yet in the dream you often know where you are and what's going on. Your memories are different from those you have in the waking world, your thoughts, your experiences, they aren't the same as the ones you have when you're awake. When you dream you know things peculiar to that particular dream, things you certainly don't know whilst awake, and much of your waking knowledge disappears in the realm of dreams. So, to what extent can we say that you're the same person whilst dreaming and waking? Don't we rather have to say that that dreamed up person, behind whose eyes you find yourself, isn't you at all? And, when you wake up, that person doesn't exist anymore, and his mind slowly fades away as you forget it. Or rather, shouldn't we say that he never existed at all, and he was only ever the product of hallucinogens in your brain?" Stephen gave a low murmur of unenthusiastic understanding. He could see what Dhiyaa was saying, but what was the point?

"There's an old Hylian legend," Dhiyaa continued, "about Koholint Island, which was in fact nothing more than an island dreamed up by the great Wind Fish as he lay slumbering at its centre. The legend says that one day the hero found his way to Koholint Island and was charged with the task of waking the Wind Fish up. He asked one of the inhabitants when they had started to live on the island. 'What do you mean by "when?"' was the native's response, 'Whoa! The concept just makes my head hurt!' Nevertheless, the hero persisted in his quest and was eventually successful in rousing the Wind Fish from his sleep. Sure enough, as soon as he did so, Koholint Island, and all the people that inhabited it, disappeared, faded away into nothing. The hero was left in the middle of the sea, clinging on to the wreckage of his ship, the Wind Fish soaring through the sky above him."

"Koholint Island?" said Stephen, his memory aroused, "that's from Zelda."

"And so what if it is? Surely ancient legends and modern videogames share the same level of veracity. The point is this: do you think any of those Koholint natives knew that they were merely figments of the Wind Fish's dream? Didn't they trust instinctively in their own existences, just as you do in yours? How do you know that you're not a figment of your own dreaming, or, for that matter, of someone else's dream, or even a character in a written fiction? How do you know you won't cease to exist as soon as some writer somewhere stops tapping away at his keyboard?"

Stephen opened his mouth to dismiss Dhiyaa's argument as ludicrous, but suddenly he wasn't so sure. The sun had dropped further down and it threw long, orange beams across the horizon, making the world around him seem a little less real. A large shadow rose up a little ahead of them, silhouetted against the streaming sun. Stephen couldn't make out what it was. In the ethereal sunbeams Stephen felt as though he himself was somehow less substantial. It almost felt as if the orange light was passing *through* him, as if he were nothing more than a vague confluence of dust and air. He seemed to glide past the great shadow, rather then walk. He held his hand up against the sunlight, to see its solidity, but he wasn't reassured.

"Well," he said, "I suppose I can't know, not for certain. But this line of inquiry is pointless. So maybe I exist, and maybe I don't, but so what? What am I supposed to do with that uncertainty?"

"Quite right, quite right," Dhiyaa said, "its all quite, quite pointless. In the end of the day, all you can really do is assume that you *are*, and continue being as you find yourself. You are, after all, who you are." So, this was the point Dhiyaa was driving at with all his pointless gibbering. He was who he was: a man, a polygamist, with an insatiable appetite for women. And he should continue being who he *was*? Stephen growled bitterly.

"Should I just pursue every woman that takes my fancy, then?" he asked. "Spend the rest of my life moving from one woman to the next, and to hell with the consequences?"

"Would that make you happy?" Stephen knew the answer without thinking.

"No," he said. No, it wouldn't. He wanted to keep them, not abandon them. He wanted to hold them tight to his chest, squeeze them, almost as if by doing so he could draw them *into* himself. He was who he was, the thought flickered through his brain. He was Lucy's lover, he was Aglaya's husband, he loved them both and the possibility of choosing between them flickered away into nothingness, because he was who he was, and who he was couldn't bear to lose either of them.

"But then," said Stephen, "what's there left for me to do?"

"I don't know," answered Dhiyaa, "to live and to suffer, I suppose. To spend every living moment consumed by an insatiable love. To walk every waking step knowing that you can never find satisfaction, that desire will perpetually burn up your insides, smouldering as you plod slowly towards the grave. And then to sleep, perchance to dream..." Dhiyaa's voice trailed off and his gaze fell unfocused into the distance. Stephen cocked his head towards him.

"Are you suggesting I kill myself?" Dhiyaa turned to look at Stephen, a wicked grin across his face.

"Only," he said slowly, "if you really want to."

Stephen snorted and continued walking onwards. The sun was very low on the horizon now, and its red beams filled Stephen's eyes. He didn't bother to shade them; instead he allowed the warm light to dominate his vision, pulling him forwards, and he drifted lazily towards the sunset. He turned back to Dhiyaa to give him his retort, but he wasn't next to him anymore. Stephen stopped and looked behind to see Dhiyaa standing beneath the shadow they'd passed a few moments earlier. Now, with the sun behind him, Stephen could see it clearly. Standing on stilts against the dark eastern sky, a whitewashed wooden building was illuminated, seeming to glow orange as it reflected the setting sunlight. It must have been pretty dark inside, however, since lights began to come to life in the windows, from which the rumble of leisurely chatter and the clinks of cutlery against plates emerged. Dhiyaa stood at the base of one of the stilts, his eyes closed, his nose upraised, breathing in deeply, clearly filling his lungs, attentively smelling. A sudden breeze carried the smell towards Stephen and he caught the whiff of thickly battered fish festering in oil, and of chips drowned in vinegar.

"Come on," said Dhiyaa with an upwards jerk of his head, "let's get some dinner." With that he began to climb the stairs that led to the chip-shop's raised entrance. Stephen sighed and followed. He grasped the handrail, hauled himself upwards and ascended the steps, climbing up into the heady, saturated air.

The Substance of Dust
Argula Rublack

Polonius Xanthes strolled along the lantern-lit street, deep in dark and twisted thought. His experiments had not been going well recently and his frustration and melancholy were rising with every waking hour. Torn between two sentiments, one moment he was alight with fierce determination, one moment drowned in catatonic aimlessness. At times like these he would often wander through the alleys, like a ghostly watchman on patrol, until his mind calmed and finally fell into a state of numbness. He would somehow find his way home and after hours of escape reawaken with sharp speckles of sunlight shining on his face. This moment had not come yet.

The substances were still bubbling in his ears, the formulas spinning in front of his eyes, the glass of the flasks touching his skin, cutting it as it burst. The stench of failure burnt in his nostrils. He could easily evoke the scene to life again, as if the moment had never passed. *Embittered fool,* a voice rose to speak. *Why not finally surrender?* At this his mind's pendulum swayed abruptly. *But, no! Surrender is impossible! I must continue. I must! ... the nonsense I believe... to conquer the power of dreams, a force so elusive and great, is not for amateurs like me...*

Now more stumbling than walking, he turned around one of the many well-known darkened corners. Exhaustion seized him and his eyes grew heavy. He was about to commence his return home when he made out a shadow in the corner of his eye. A black figure was sitting on the cobblestones just a few dozen footsteps away. Screwing up his eyes as he approached, he could make out nothing. *You are tired, Polonius, you are imagining things...*

You are not.

He flinched as the figure took shape. Foggy shadows cloaked its statue, making it resemble a cloud of smoke rather than a living creature. Feet of broken claws, webbed hands and tangled, snake-like hair were its only distinguishable features. But it was above all its eyes that drew Polonius in against all his better instinct – two dark red beads sown into two hollow eye sockets.

Coming to a halt in front of the creature, he demanded: "What are you?"

The creature's mouth curled into a mocking smile. *You do not know? I am disappointed.*

Polonius remained silent.

You do not answer? I indeed am disappointed. The being raised itself from the ground and shifted menacingly in Polonius' direction.

He backed away, just to hit the wall, suddenly inexplicably terrified. *Oh God, this must be a dream... It must be. Can I not distinguish anymore? I have gone mad!*

The being screeched with laughter. *Fool! Fool! You are not mad! You are the purpose of my wanderings. Take this!* It presented a small leather bag from the nothingness of its shape. *Take it. TAKE IT!*

With a sharp gasp, Polonius awoke to the speckles of sunlight stinging in his eyes. Frozen he lay under his blanket. He began to shiver. A nightmare, he told himself. Probably it was the new substances he had acquired. They might have had side-effects after usage. Slowly, he made himself sit upright and clenched his fists to control the shaking as the dream slowly faded from his consciousness. After he had calmed himself, he rose.

The dream had been fearsome to him, but the break of day was even more so. He dreaded what he had experienced over and over again in the past years of his life. Countless fruitless days and nights of work. He knew the only option was to accept the limitations imposed. He needed to refocus his studies, instead of expecting success when challenging the impossible. The knowledge of what could not be accomplished would have to be enough.

Intending to consult his library he walked past his table stacked to the brink with distillation devices, bags of powders, jars of fluid and manuscripts filled with endless riddles of annotation. As his

The Substance of Dust

gaze slid past his little cell, it fell on something that had not been there the day before. A leather bag sat quietly on a heap of books piled on the table. It was not one of the many he already possessed and had used so many times that their colour had faded, yet it seemed vaguely familiar.

He took the pouch and tugged loose the strings closing it to inspect what it contained. Not recognizing it, he carefully took out a pinch of the contents. It felt soft, slightly sandy and shone silvery in the light gliding into the room from the small window. Like dust.

Polonius could not remember where he had got it from or the use he had intended for it. He wondered how he could have forgotten. He closed the bag, placed it in his pocket and proceeded to read one of the books lying open on the table instead. After a dozen page turns, a knock interrupted.

"Enter," Polonius said. In came a young boy, around the age of fourteen, carrying a thickly-woven sack on his shoulder, which he immediately threw on the ground with a strained sigh. Polonius took out his pocket watch – three minutes past the hour. He turned in his chair and eyed the boy disapprovingly. "Be careful, Ciro. There are valuable materials in there. And besides, you are late," he said with unconstrained annoyance in his tone. The boy did not answer and pulled the bundle over to the table to unpack it. Polonius returned to his book, but eventually rested a watchful eye on the boy. "Ciro" he finally addressed him, "today you will read those documents over there. Memorize them by the time the sun goes down." He pointed vaguely into a corner with a single dripping candle beside a pile of papers. Ciro looked dismayed but reluctantly conceded: "Yes, Master Xanthes."

The coming hours were spent in silence except for the occasional questions Ciro hesitantly murmured across the room followed by curt answers by his tutor. The silence of dripping wax and rustling documents brought Polonius back to his own obsessive questionings. Refusing to leave him be, no matter how much he tried to dismiss them, they made him prepare formulas and experiments before his mind's eye with those small alterations that might change everything.

"Master Xanthes," Ciro suddenly chimed in. "Do you really believe it is true that alchemists can bring dreams to life?"

"No," Polonius answered immediately and definitely.
"But you made a note besides these..."
"I told you it is impossible. My research has shown it."
The wax could be heard dripping again.
"But..."
"Listen, boy." Polonius turned around abruptly, glaring dangerously and spit with venom: "Dreams are but immaterial manifestations of our mind at sleep, nonsensical delusions, impossible ideals at best – as is, of course, the nature of the ideal – the substance of which is nothing but the mere dust at your feet." Ciro dared not object again.

~

Ciro left in the last lights of sunset after a moderately successful quizzing by his tutor who was now left to himself again. He was tired from the hours of reading by flickering candlelight. Despite this he forced himself to stay awake. His mind suddenly strayed back to the leather bag from earlier and the dust within. Something told him that it had a significance he could not grasp. But more likely it was one of Ciro's vain attempts to spite him. He quickly dismissed the matter under this conclusion before returning to write further notes.

You convinced yourself that the bag contains mere dust, did you not?

Polonius' pen slipped a loud scratch on the paper. "Who said that?" he demanded.

You will find, the same voice continued, *that it is far more than that*

Polonius' eyes dashed to find the speaker. Then he heard footsteps. Behind him. He jumped out of his chair and turned to find a creature hulled in peculiar ragged garments walking towards him, eyes glowing red in their hollow depths. *That bag,* it said, *contains the substance to awaken dreams to life.*

Polonius' face slipped. But soon he regained his composure. Whatever or whoever this was in front of him, it was surely playing tricks on him. "I have no time for your nonsense," he growled and forced himself to turn away.

Says the man whose wish it is to cross the boundary of dream and reality. The unknown being sniggered. Polonius' attention returned to it. "How do you know?" he uttered unbelievingly.

It is hardly surprising that someone strolling through the streets at night, mumbling like a mad man, would be noticed. Besides, I have been watching you, Polonius. I find you very interesting.

"How do you know my name?"

What difference does it make?

Polonius' hair stood up on the back of his neck. No one was supposed to know. How could this being know?

Do not fret. I am the only one who bothers with you, it said as if reading his mind. *I alone see the potential that others do not.*

"You are a fool if you believe in my potential," Polonius heard himself saying, not sure why he is responding in the first place. "I am nothing but an independent researcher as you say and I am quite happy to continue to be such."

I merely request that you put to use what you have been given, the mighty weapon that lies in your hands. Its glowing eyes focused on the leather bag dug away in the pocket. Warily Polonius stepped away. "I have no time for this. I hold no mighty weapon in my hands, nor am I striving for such. I intend to do my research in peace and quiet. Now if you will…"

Such is the talk of fools, Polonius. And you are no fool. You know of the powers hidden in this world. Powers you can harness for your use. The figure's mouth of shadow extended to what might have resembled a grin. *You would not simply research, would you? That is not the reason why you are working so hard, is it? You want to use what you will find.*

Polonius grew increasingly uneasy in this creature's presence. He was sure that it was dangerous, that he should not believe it, never mind talk to it. Yet he knew what kept him standing there. But if he allowed himself to be immersed in this fantastical talk, the perilous way he had been willing to choose once might become too tempting again, more so than it already was.

He shook himself and walked briskly outside slamming the door behind him. The being did not follow. On his aimless walk under the setting sun his mind was racing. *I am such a fool. I have already been infected by its talk.*

"To awaken dreams to life," he whispered under his breath, clutching the bag of dust tightly in his pocket. "To conquer the power of dreams."

~

The shards cut deeper this time.

Polonius hissed angrily and withdrew his bleeding palm. Traces of dirty silver shine sticking to his fingers mixed with the trickling blood. He stood up and in his fury kicked the chair he had sat on for hours as the candles had burnt down, wasted. What fatuous notion had led him to think there was a chance of dust magically providing him what he had sought for years?

As he bandaged his hand exhaustion crept over him. He shuffled towards his bed and fell asleep as he landed on the rough cloth.

He felt himself sinking. His eyes closed, deep darkness encapsulated him. The feeling of being drawn into the deep did not strike him as odd at first. It was rather welcoming. Then in a flash, his senses awakened. Cold water! All around him! He was drowning!

He struggled against the heavy blue as salty water filled his lungs. How he reached the top he did not know but he had never been so glad to be spluttering, coughing, breathing. After rubbing his eyes he found himself facing a grassy bank. It was near nightfall. He was trapped in the body of boyhood again. And he was being called for.

"Polonius, come, enough play for today. We are going home." His mother's voice. Although his mind alerted him that she was long dead, her existence seemed so natural that he followed. He swam on shore and approached the two figures of his parents. They were blurry, unclear – he had forgotten their faces long ago. His mind only visualized the ornaments they wore. His father's pocket watch, which he always carried with him, and his mother's necklace laced with red beads, now hidden at the bottom of a chest in his study.

Silently his mother took his hand and the family strolled off together. The road was steep and uneven. The black night made it impossible to see the stones tumbling beneath one's feet. The boy –

The Substance of Dust

his former self – was tense as if he knew, even without the knowledge of his present self, that tragedy would strike.

His dream vividly recalled his memory. Torrents of rain building to a storm. His parents rushing under a tree, that accursed tree, to wait until the worst was over. He had fallen asleep, only to awaken to the wails of his father, begging the gods to have mercy. His mother lying, dying, poisoned by the vicious snake he never saw. The only evidence remaining – two beads of blood on her leg, matching those around her neck. Young Polonius frightened, not understanding, his mother's last shrill screech of pain ringing in his ear.

His eyes shot open. Grown Polonius had returned to his underground cage on a winter night. Snow was floating down from the sky, through the small window, onto his blanket and pillow. Shivering he got up in search for a warming fire. The room seemed damper and colder than usual. The depth of its darkness seemed impenetrable. From this front of blackness, a figure emerged. The strange being of shadow had returned.

"You!" exclaimed Polonius. "What do you want? Speak!"

It did not respond.

Polonius stood there a while, not daring to advance. Gathering his courage, he finally uttered: "You have pestered me enough, creature. Be gone!"

The creature's hairs hissed at this unacceptable command but its mouth remained sealed and merely curled to a smile. The silence of falling snow had been replaced by a constant thundering. Polonius turned to witness the weather's new spectacle. Hail stones were skating and jumping into his room.

"Is this your doing?" Polonius confronted the creature, his voice trembling. The being stretched out its webbed hand and with it cut through the air sharply. The thundering ceased and silence returned. The hail stones melted, only leaving small puddles covering the floor.

Then it snipped its fingers and presented its hand. A red bead dropped from the ceiling and fell into its palm. Polonius turned his head upwards. Hundreds of beads were falling through the cracks in the stone. Soon their tapping and bouncing on the ground was all around him. "Stop this immediately!" he yelled. But again the creature only gave a mute response.

Helpless Polonius curled up and tried to shield his head with his arms. The red of the beads was slowly filling the wet ground, covering his reflection. But it could not conceal what he had yet failed to notice. Where his eyes should have been only two hollow sockets remained for the red beads to fill them. Polonius screamed.

~

As the rising sun crept over the sky Ciro made his usual way up the hill from the town to his tutor's remote residence. With every new ray enlightening his vision the boy dreaded descending down into that cold and murky basement more and more. But as his father said, it was good to nurture his talents. Ciro himself was not so sure. And the ardour of studying with a man such as Xanthes did not seem worth the effort. His moody and ruminative nature, his constant scolding and harshly curt answers to questions were infuriating. Ciro thought it surprising that there seemed to be a grudging respect left for him in the town, so no one minded the eccentric and misanthropic character lodging in that far off place in the neighbourhood. No one, therefore, would bother to oppose his place of study.

Sighing heavily as he approached the stone stairs down to his daily prison, Ciro once again gave in to his fate, the better knowledge of others. But as he entered through the wooden door, he knew something was awry.

Xanthes was sitting in his chair as usual but no paper was stirring, no candle had been lighted. His master was just sitting there, frozen to a statue. "Master Xanthes?" Ciro asked unsurely.

The statue jerked into life at the sound of a human voice. A terrified yet exhilarated face turned to Ciro. The grotesque sight was enough for Ciro to shrink back behind the door.

Polonius, becoming aware of the world around him again, let his eyes hastily skim the room. Noticing a small bag next to him, he snatched it, put it into his pocket and attempted to regain his composure. "Ciro," he started and paused a while as if he had forgotten something. He then drew out his pocket watch and finally commented: "You are not late today."

The rest of the day was spent in a most oppressive and tense atmosphere. Except for Polonius' occasional mumblings as he sat bent over his desk clutching something tightly in his hand, which Ciro could not see, no sounds filled the room. Ciro was too afraid of his tutor's odd humour to pose any question and remained bent over his assigned book at all times. He was very glad when he finally was dismissed.

But Polonius halted him before he could clutch the door handle. "Ciro," he began. "You asked me yesterday if alchemists could bring dreams to life. In the eventuality that you would possess such power what would you use it for?"

Ciro looked puzzled and with an edge of annoyance on his voice, he said: "You told me that it is impossible. Why would I consider the eventuality?"

"Merely as a method to exercise your brain," was the reply.

Ciro thought a while. "I don't know. We do not choose what we dream. It is... random, mostly a useless line of images and impressions. It would depend on what would come to life out of the dream..." He paused again.

Polonius nodded and dropped his head. "Indeed," he mumbled absent-mindedly and then waved his hand towards his pupil. "Send my greetings to your father. You can go home now."

Ciro grimaced. "I will."

After the door clanked shut Polonius retreated back into his muddle of thoughts. He sat down on his chair, staring blankly at the two red beads in his palm. As soon as he had discovered these after he awoke, he had run to his chest and dug deep into its contents until he found his mother's necklace. But it had been intact. Complete. The two additional beads had either appeared out of nowhere or... manifested themselves into the real world out of his dream. He had examined both types of beads next to each other. They were exactly the same. It could not be coincidence.

The fragile dream, the longed-for impossible, had become reality. It must have been related to the dusty substance as the creature from his dreams had told him. It was the only thing that could have changed the circumstances so much. But why did it have the effect it had, what had activated it? As matters stood his years of studies were rendered useless. No basis, no control. He had no other choice but to experiment. The thought alone kindled terror in him.

That night Polonius lay awake, afraid to fall asleep, clutching the two beads tightly in his hand. He was not foolish enough to believe that he could forever flee from that inevitable human need, but his conscious mind still tried to jolt himself back into the light every time his eyes closed ready to drift off into sleep. What would happen to him if he finally did not have any choice but to give in? How could he transform more from dream to reality without knowing how and with what consequence? He thought of the creature that had been haunting him. He was sure that it harboured the key to the mystery. The fogs of his memory were calling out to him that he should remember something, not long ago, connected to the being. But he was too tired. A curtain of darkness surrounded him as he closed his eyes.

Soon he found himself walking in a dimly lit corridor with a line of doors at each side. This place was strangely familiar to him. Stepping towards one of the doors, he opened it. Beyond it was nothing, just a dark wooden wall. The same wall appeared behind the next three doors. The fifth door revealed a room without windows coated in the greens of woollen carpet and tapestry, lit only by a fireplace. On the mantelpiece Polonius found his watch again, an omen of its owner's absence. In the middle of the shady green lay a boy, curled up with an open book next to him. Polonius entered the room. His steps were smothered by the smooth surface, as he went towards the boy. The child did not stir. Quietly Polonius picked up the book and examined it. It was a storybook, filled with ink paintings swirling between the letters. An alchemist was depicted, abstractly forming mystical creatures from the clouds of smoke surrounding him. Creating his own world filled with his vivid, wild dreams.

He looked up to place the book back next to the child. It had awoken. Two pairs of identical grey eyes were staring at each other. But the child's eyes were soon averted by an approaching presence behind his back. Polonius did not need to turn around to understand. "I should have known this to be one of your scams," he hissed angrily.

The Substance of Dust

You accuse me? The creature chuckled. *These are your dreams, Polonius. I have no control over them. I can merely choose to appear in whichever dream you happen to dream. And my, is it not fascinating what one can learn about you in them?*

Polonius glared dangerously. "You believe you can deduce knowledge about me from the fantasies that spring from my mind at sleep? How foolish."

You of all people should know the power that dreams harbour, Polonius. It is the gift of humans to imagine the impossible. That child, it pointed at Polonius' young self, *was always a dreamer. Great mind, great imagination! I'm sure its grown form has not changed much even though bitter experience and disappointment have tinged it.*

"Stop trying to convince me of this madness. This is merely a dream, something of no consequence. Your talk is useless."

I offer you what you have sought for all your life, even before you wished to bring back those in the realm of the dead. Why will you not use what you have finally obtained?

Polonius could feel the beads weighing heavily in his tightened fist. "The dead cannot be revived. Nor can other non-existent entities just suddenly appear. It goes against all the principles of nature and science, all I have studied over the years," he forced himself to say.

You close your eyes from your long sought goal so easily? Were the beads not evidence enough?

Polonius shivered as he saw his reflection in the red of its eyes. They would not accept further denial. "Yes. Yes, but... I am afraid," he confessed.

So doubtful even though it lies right in front of you? I am tired of trying to persuade you with words, Polonius. Actions must follow. The being strutted towards Polonius and grabbed his wrist. Polonius let out a yelp as the two red beads dropped out of his hand. *I will have to demonstrate.*

But the monster did not fulfil its threat. Instead it paused, still grasping Polonius' hand. Then its grip tightened with anger. *You fool! I thought you understood!*

"What do you mean?" The pressure on his wrist was growing painful, making him wince. In the back of his mind he was vaguely aware of a strange humming, disturbing his thoughts.

You had everything prepared yesterday. Why not today? Are you trying to play games with me, you puny human? snarled the creature.

"I don't understand," cried Polonius. "What did I not prepare? What did I not understand?" The humming was growing louder. He thought he could distinguish a voice within it. His name, being shouted out by someone. The creature's outlines, the room around them and the voice were becoming fainter as green faded into black.

The preparation of the dust! The creature was yelling at him but he could hardly hear it. *You...*

"Master Xanthes!"

Polonius shot up from his bed. Ciro inhaled sharply at the abrupt movement and jumped backwards. But Polonius did not notice. The room around him was spinning and his head was aching. He felt like he was going to be ill as he pressed his hands against his temples to ineffectually lessen the dizziness. His wrist stung painfully.

"Master Xanthes... are you alright?" Ciro approached his tutor timidly.

"What in all seven hells are you doing here?" Polonius mumbled, slowly remembering to grasp onto the threads of his fading dream. It had been important, he had to remember.

"I... the sun has already risen. I came here for my instruction but you were still asleep." Polonius now became aware of the sunlight falling into the room. How had he not woken up earlier? Then suddenly the memory returned as Ciro continued: "You seemed like... you were having a bad dream. You were in turmoil. So, I thought it might be best to wake you."

Polonius stared at his student, incredulous. Then his features twisted into an infuriated grimace. "That is what you thought, did you? You imbecile!" he roared.

"But I..."

"I don't care what you thought! How dare you wake me?" Polonius jumped up and shoved Ciro aside. "So close, so close, damn everything!" he mumbled violently as he paced the room. "Letting me believe I am so close and then removing me from it indefinitely again. Cursed, that is what I am." His fists slammed on the table letting papers fly through the air.

The Substance of Dust

Ciro shifted his feet nervously. "I'm sorry. I did not mean to…"

"You did not mean to what? Wake me? Although that is exactly what you just said you intended to do? Do you take me for a fool to believe such empty words? I would rather you had killed me!"

"But… I'm sure you don't mean that…"

"Mean, mean, what does anything mean?" Polonius spat. "Get out of here!"

With a pained face Ciro ran for the door, slamming it behind him. As his rage evaporated Polonius slumped into his chair and buried his face in his hands. What had he not understood? Why could he not understand?

It was only habit that forced him to light a candle. He took the bag with the substance and the two red beads out of his pocket and held one in one hand, one in the other. After a while his brows knitted. He dropped the beads onto the papers covering the table. Then he opened the bag and examined the dust again. He took a pinch between his fingers and rubbed them together. His eyes returned to the beads. He picked one of them up with the same two fingers.

Then he finally understood.

~

"Well, Ciro, you can hardly blame Polonius for his rage. Waking him, what were you thinking? It is rather inappropriate to behave like that." His father's imposing figure stood looking out of the window, arms folded behind his back, while Ciro sullenly cowered in his chair. He felt his stern gaze even as it wasn't pointed in his direction. After Ciro had fled Xanthes' house he had run straight to his father to demand that he would never have to return to that horrible place ever again. Now he regretted doing so. "You will return to him immediately and apologize for your insolence."

"But, father…" Ciro attempted but he was interrupted: "You have stated your complaints quite clearly, I do not need a repeated hearing of them, Ciro. Now return to your studies."

"Can't someone else be my tutor? I'm sure there are others who could teach me."

His father sighed heavily. "I have explained before that I believe you are in the best of hands with Polonius. I know he can seem very strange, and that he can be moody and quick to anger. But he is a very clever man."

"A clever man maybe, but certainly not a very nice one," Ciro mumbled grudgingly.

His father's face stiffened. "Ciro, you do realize you are talking about an old friend of mine."

"Why should I suffer at the hands your old acquaintances?" Ciro bit his lip, almost immediately regretting what he had said.

"Because I demand you to do so. And you will not ever again disrespect any old acquaintance of mine, is that understood?" His father's voice remained calm but Ciro could feel the growing anger bubbling in it. Every further argument was pointless. He knew his pleas would be in vain. He lowered his head and reluctantly conceded: "Yes, father."

He stood up and turned to leave, when his father halted him: "How is he?"

Ciro grimaced. "The usual. Well, not quite. He seems to have had trouble with sleeping recently. More than usual, that is."

His father turned to the window again but Ciro could sense the worried look on his face. "It is not unusual as you say." The unsaid lay heavily in the air. Ciro, of course, knew what his father was thinking of. Of the brilliant young man he had met at university who had never been the same again when his old childhood foolery had taken over his studies. Of the broken man who had been left alone with his impossible goal. Of how not even he, his friend, could understand him anymore, even though he had tried. Of the deal struck reluctantly to retain even the slightest connection between two men who had long ago gone separate ways. That burden he, Ciro, had never asked for yet still felt an odd sense of duty to take it upon him. He clenched his teeth angrily as he felt himself soften towards that strange friend of his father again. Of course he would return to that alien yet so familiar man. Because it was what his conscience demanded.

"I will see you later, father." Ciro mumbled into the silence and closed the door behind him.

The Substance of Dust

~

Everything was prepared. He sipped the tincture that would let him immediately fall asleep again. A phial of his blood mixed with the substance was placed in his hand. Eagerly he stared at his pocket watch. A few more minutes and the potion would release its effect. Already he began to feel the welcomed heaviness of sleep. Exhilarated, he closed his eyes.

He only had to enter the world of dreams again. He hoped with his innermost that he would finally succeed, that the labour would finally be worthwhile. He would have given anything for it.

~

Ciro stepped through the door to find the complete chaos created in his short absence. Candles had been toppled, leaving the wax dropping to the floor, books had been flung from the shelves, the documents were even more scattered than usual. Gulping down a lump in his throat with his inner inhibition to step further, Ciro looked around for his master. He found him lying on the stone floor, limbs outstretched, a phial in his hand. He quietly crept closer.

"Master Xanthes?" He was asleep. Again! Unsure of what to do Ciro nervously searched the room but he was clueless as to what he was looking for. The whole situation was so odd; like a bad dream.

~

Polonius opened his eyes to a storm-tossed sky. He was floating in black clouds. Nothing else was about him but smashing rain, glaring lightning and the growl of thunder. Polonius cursed the uncontrollable nature of dreams. He needed some kind of material, an object. That would be much easier. It had been done before, it could be done again.

Step out of that carnival, Polonius. To me.

Polonius was no longer surprised at the creature's presence. He stepped through the storm front towards it. The dissonance was left behind and an eerie silence spread in its stead.

The creature's and Polonius's eyes met, grey on red.

I assume you have made your preparations this time.
The corner of Polonius's mouth shifted to a crooked grin. "Of course."

~

Ciro searched the materials scattered over the table urgently. He might be punished for his actions but somehow he knew he had to wake his tutor before it was too late. A part of him still wondered why he was making the effort. But he continued nonetheless.

He skimmed through Xanthes' documents. Most were incoherent scribbling he could not understand. He took up fluids, powders, read all the labels. Nothing made sense. His eye then fell on a small bag. He vaguely remembered it. Xanthes had been trying to hide it from him the other day, or so he believed. He let his hand slip into the bag and held what he removed towards the candlelight to examine it. It was only a silvery-grey dust. "Useless." he muttered, frustrated.

At that moment Xanthes clenched his teeth and started breathing heavily. Ciro panicked. It was starting again, just like this morning. He must be sick. And he, Ciro, needed to act, to help him. But what could he do when he knew so little?

~

You insolent human! Are you really this dim? the creature growled as its webbed hands locked around Polonius's throat. The snakes on its head hissed in an angry chorus.

"Why? I had everything this time, I…" croaked Polonius, struggling for breath.

Silent! Its sharp-clawed feet lashed out. Polonius cried out hoarsely. His legs were burning as warm blood ran out of his wounds. *Or you will whimper no more.*

~

As the blood started flowing Ciro screamed, terrified. The wounds had appeared out of nowhere. What was happening? What was this terrible power? His instincts were telling him to run. His mind shouted at him to move, to do something. But he just stood there, petrified.

Then his tutor let out a scream in his sleep. Ciro leaped back in fear and fell. Just in time, he supported himself with both his arms to stop falling flat on his back. His hands stung and burnt as he hit the ground. He had cut himself. Ciro turned his head to find shards of glass lying on the ground. He bit his lip as he looked at his hurt hands. Blood was trickling out of the cuts mixed with a dusty silver shine.

~

Suddenly the monster loosened his grip and let Polonius slip from it. Polonius coughed and gasped for air as he tried to stand on his wounded leg.

When he had regained enough air, he looked up to the being. It was standing there, silently, its head turned to the side, red eyes glowering. Then it smiled its ghastly, shadowy smile. *Oh, my dear Polonius,* it whispered, *you clever, clever man.*

An instant later, Polonius had returned to lying on the cold stone floor. Confused he let his eyes adjust to its familiar surroundings. Had the dust had its effect, had something changed?

But what he perceived made him doubt that he had returned to normality. He glanced at Ciro, lying on the floor next to him, sickly pale and unmoving, a red puddle surrounding him.

"Dear God, Ciro!" Polonius exclaimed as he shifted onto his knees and bent down to examine his pupil. He felt his pulse – weak – and forced his eyes open – dazed. Blood loss. But he could not find any other wounds except the cuts on the boy's hand. The amount of blood flowing was far too much for such a minor injury. He examined the wound more closely. Silver shone out of the red.

"I had not expected a human sacrifice. I must confess, it seems that I have judged wrongly, my friend."

Polonius gazed in terror as the nightmarish being came alive. The blood slithered along the floor to create a bundle of shadows. With every trickle soaked up a further part of its body emerged – the same webbed hands and claws, the same snake-like hair and glowing red eyes.

"No. Stop. Ciro, wake up!" Polonius uttered frantically between clenched teeth as he pressed his hands around Ciro's fingers to stop the blood running. But it was useless – Ciro's blood was in direct contact with the substance. Polonius cursed himself for not realizing earlier. Now he could not stop it. Meanwhile the creature became ever more manifest. Ever more real.

"This was not your intention? Never mind, it will not change anything." The creature raised its hand towards the snakes on its head. One of them lashed out and it quickly withdrew its hand before the bite. It smiled, pleased. "So this is what... being alive feels like. How exhilarating!" It burst out into a joyous laugh.

Ciro meanwhile had grown pale as snow – frozen, without a drop of life remaining. Polonius stared at his pupil in disbelief. It was incomprehensible, impossible. He began to tremble. Hastily he shifted away from the corpse. "But..." he began and then yelled in despair: "But it was just a dream! A dream, nothing of consequence, of importance! Not real! How could I have known..."

"Denial, is it?" The creature growled. "Don't be a fool, Polonius. You knew."

"No, I would never..." But he knew he would have. Before, in his desperate, unthinking madness. How could he explain that he was responsible for the death of his only friend's son? How could he live with it?

"Oh, Polonius, my friend, what is one life compared to this? You have done it! The dream, the creature of your imagination, finally entered the real world. And I am finally where I want to be. Our contract is fulfilled."

"Contract? I never made a contract with you, vile creature!" shouted Polonius enraged.

"Call it contract, silent agreement, mutual understanding, what does it matter?" hissed the being and stared in marvel at itself. "I had everything, even a body – but no blood." It smiled. "It was the final ingredient I needed and you provided it. I am finally alive. Not dependent anymore on you and your mind at sleep."

Polonius shivered. Partners in crime – he would not accept that truth. He heaved himself from the floor and grasped the table's edge

The Substance of Dust

for support as he unstably stood on his injured leg. "You don't belong here. You have no right to be here. You will go back and never return! And you will bring Ciro back!" he yelled.

The creature laughed. "What nonsense. You believe you can command me? And besides, I am no miracle worker, Polonius. I cannot bring back the dead. It is not possible, as you correctly guessed."

"But he... he was..."

The creature snarled. "What is this sudden change of sentiment, you ungrateful worm?"

Polonius clenched his teeth in pain and rage. He seized the bag with the dust in it from the table and flung it into the fire. It immediately caught flame and fell to ashes. Before the anger settled and the shock of what he had just done sunk in, he shouted, "There! It's gone! I do not need your tricks!" The creature's beady eyes almost revealed the expression of disbelief. But even more so of grim disappointment. "I should never have allowed myself to be seduced by your scheme. My conscience should not have allowed it!"

"Your conscience makes you a coward!" the monster spat. "You humans and your sentimentality and moral codes. It is meaningless, imposed tyranny, no more. Contrary to my belief, you are no better than others, Polonius. I've had enough of you."

The snakes hissed hungrily at the alchemist. Polonius lowered his head, awaiting the poisonous sting. But he heard the scratching of claws along the floor instead as the being turned to leave. "Wait, where are you going?" called Polonius after it.

"That is not your concern," it said and stepped out of the door into the light. Polonius tried to follow but his leg would not support him and he fell onto the glass splinters strayed across the floor.

As he lay there, quiet and still, not minding the pain of the new cuts, Ciro's drained body in front of his eyes, the fire cackling as if its recent consumption had pleased it, realization crushed him. So many years, his life's work, wasted; a worthless, cruel sacrifice. Nothing remained. Nothing but piles of useless paper and equipment in this cell of floating dust brightened by the sun. He cried to dream again. To amend what had been done wrong. But it was too late.

~

The rain of the windy night pelted against the tavern's swinging lantern. A lone traveller limped to cower underneath it and knock on the door. He was ushered into the dry by the barkeep soon after. "Horrible night to be out there, my friend." The traveller nodded silently. "What brings you here?" the barkeep addressed him again. "I am just passing by," stated the murmured reply. "Well, have yourself a seat, I'll fetch something to warm you up." The stranger declined and asked to be given a room for the night instead.

After having been shown to his lodging, the traveller sank wearily onto the bed. His dishevelled appearance, weary look in his grey eyes and ashen colour made him seem much older than his age. He gloomily stared at the rain covered windowpane. "Why in all seven hells did I come back after all this time?" he muttered to himself.

The next morning he left for the roads leading outside town before the sun had risen. After a slow and long walk, he arrived at a small stone hut which seemed to have fallen into disuse for several years. He struggled towards an entrance at the side of it, leading down into a cellar. He opened the door. What he found was familiar yet changed. Animals and travellers had made it their temporary home, had left remnants of their occupation and taken from the old. Smudged broken glass was still strayed among the occasional weeds growing out of the stone floor. All the candles had been taken, only occasional dots of wax had stayed. Whatever wood there had been had been burnt by the flames lighted in the fireplace and lay now in scattered ashes. Many books and manuscripts had disappeared. Those that remained lay scattered, ripped and moulding.

The traveller's face betrayed no emotion as he limped into the room. As he silently let his eyes wander over the scene he asked himself: "What did I hope to find in this godforsaken place?"

"I see you have returned." The man winced and turned his head. A creature of shadow stepped beside him. "You took your time. I have been waiting for you, Polonius."

"Waited for me?" Polonius repeated without understanding. Silence fell between the alchemist and the being.

"This world of yours," the creature started finally, "it is not worth living in. I believed you humans put to flesh what in my world was only a mere non-existing shadow. It is peculiar that you pride yourselves in being alive but spend your fleeting days doing nothing of purpose. Your imaginations never come to fruition. You do not even remember them, you assign no significance to them. And if you do, it is so, so imperfect." It snarled in bitter discontent. "I would rather return to a world where all is nothing than be confronted with this constant disappointment."

"So that was your quest?" Polonius asked astonished.

"You might call it that," it confirmed.

"And it has come to an end?"

"I cannot return without the dust." The creature eyed him knowingly. As if a silent command guided him, Polonius let his hand wander to his pocket. Out came a familiar bag, one he had held many times in contemplation and temptation. The creature smiled darkly. "I thought you would gather the remains."

Polonius looked towards the floor, ashamed of his own predictability. He had not been able to give up on it completely, even though he had never dared to use it.

"So I can end this misery. Now." The being impatiently stretched out its hand.

Polonius quickly pulled away, clutching the bag tighter. "I have a request," he said firmly.

The snakes presented their fangs and snatched for the dust but the creature halted them and they slid back again. Polonius took a deep breath and said: "Take me with you."

More angry hissing and snapping. The being's red eyes flared up dangerously. "What makes you think you have the right to request such a thing?"

"I am one of the fools who wasted their fleeting lives. I achieved nothing. I only destroyed." He lowered his head. Absent-mindedly he drew his pocket watch from his coat and for a while watched it announce how late it was and how the seconds were ticking away. "I chased something I could never have. Not in this world." He lifted his gaze to look the creature straight into the beady eyes. "If I do not go with you now, I will die and fade to…" he paused.

"Dust?" it suggested.

Polonius chuckled humourlessly. "Yes, dust."

After a long while of contemplation the creature said: "I will grant your request."

Polonius smiled as he handed over the small leather bag. Then he looked down upon his watch again.

It had stopped.

Dream Story
Anissa Putois

I stepped off the bus. As it had stopped right on the pedestrian crossing I had to circle it to reach the opposite pavement of the crowded Euston road, and as I did so, I noticed a poster on the bus's side for the second Twilight film. Didn't that one come out ages ago? I took a closer look. Ah, it was an ad for the blue-ray version. My musings regarding what on earth blu-ray actually was were put on hold as I caught the seductive scent of the corner pasta shop. It drew me in.

Proudly swinging the paper bag containing my freshly bought 'Cheese Please' pasta with extra olives, I exited the shop and walked home, forgetting all about Twilight and blu-ray.

Once home I poured the contents of the cardboard box into a bowl, peppered it extravagantly, wolfed it down with two cups of tea, and went to bed.

I fell into a quiet sleep. Quiet? Or so I thought.

~

We stood backed against a corner, my mother and I, dressed in chequered shirts and corduroy pants. We may have shared Bella's dress sense, but these were no friendly vampires we were up against. Four shapes stood in front of us, they wore tight zip-up jackets and dark trousers. It was hard to tell whether they were male or female. A sudden instinct came over me: it was time to attack. I jumped in the air, my mother close behind me, at least four feet above our enemies' heads. As I drew my sharp claws in preparation for the fatal blow, the four silhouettes bounced up as high as us and stood, suspended in mid-air, their indistinct faces threatening us. I assumed they were vampires, like us, though my version was a little different from the usual tales of our generation's vampire craze. There was no blood, no fangs, and no sappy love stories. Trapped in the air by the menacing shapes, our strength seemingly equal but their numbers twice ours, I realised the fight was hopeless.

~

That second cup of tea might have been a mistake. Half asleep I stumbled out of bed. When I returned, feeling lighter, I groggily snickered at the oddity of my dream. I fell back to sleep, having no idea what the rest of the night had in store for me.

~

I gazed out, resting my elbows on the windowsill (probably exhausted after all that vampire-fighting). I seemed to be on the top-story of a tall brick building, staring down at the main street of a Spanish village. On either side of the street below stood small, one-story high wooden barracks, with swinging doors reminiscent of Western movies. Just like the set of a Western, the barracks were raised on stages, and the ground between them was rust-brown sand. A warm breeze blew through my hair as I watched the villagers below, sensing their state of frenzy over an apparently imminent attack.

With a swirl the scene changed. I found myself at street level, holding up a bicycle with a puppy in the front basket, and accepting the guard of a small child. My mission, it seemed, was to take the child out of the perilous town to a countryside boarding school. My father and grandfather saw me off, the latter handing me a bag of mini-croissants for sustenance.

I rode off, the kid running in front of me. But all of a sudden I panicked, the child had gotten away, as had the puppy and the till now deserted countryside had morphed into a busy Bombay street, bull-carts and motorbikes whizzing by us (more whizzing done by the bikes than the bull-carts). Jumping off my bike, I tucked the puppy under one arm, my fingers tightly gripping the precious mini-croissants, and grabbed the child with my other hand, running through the traffic, ultimately completing my mission and bringing them both to the safety of the remote boarding school.

~

Keys jingled noisily in the front door lock. I checked my phone: 2 a.m. My flatmate, probably coming home from a late night out, rowdily shushed whoever she had brought home with her and stumbled to the kitchen. At least three voices started cackling loudly, accompanied by the clinking of mugs. I groaned into my pillow, I had really wanted to find out what happened after the boarding school. And if those mini-croissants were any good. The chase after the child through the traffic had been so vivid! Perhaps an effect of all the pepper I had added to my dinner. My ears gradually growing accustomed to the nightly disturbance, I slipped back into a peaceful slumber.

~

Picking up my duvet once again, I rubbed at the unusual marks with my thumb, but they would not come off. It seemed my flatmate had left a note for me, scribbled in huge blue swerving ink letters on my white duvet. As I tried to read the words, they kept morphing into something different. I gave up. It seemed like such an unlikely thing for my usually dependable flatmate to do. I stormed out of my room to find her and confront her about her insolent defacing of my sleeping equipment, but I stopped in my tracks, stunned at the sight in front of me. Our usual small, dimly lit hallway had been replaced by a large shower room. My first thought was that if it weren't for the front door being right there, it would be a great bathroom. It also seemed to have become the living room, as we all sat down, my three flatmates and I, our backs to the side of the tub, and shared our life secrets.

~

Pfff. That was too much of a ridiculous thought to sleep through. Our life secrets, pah! My dreaming subconscious is very idealistic. Also it's really hot in here. I kicked off my duvet and got up to turn the radiator off. I glanced at my phone: 4:32 am. Too sleepy to cover myself properly I lazily threw myself diagonally under the duvet, my feet popping out, and resumed my dreaming.

~

I was seated on an armchair at the Western point of what seemed to be a paradisiacal island. On my left a white sandy beach stretched out in a semi-circle around a pool of turquoise sea. In the armchair opposite me an old man resembling Gandalf the Grey sat, dressed in a pale grey cloak, his long beard almost reaching the floor. He appeared to be in the middle of explaining a tricky mission that I would have to undertake. I seem to dream a lot about assignments and operations. I must fancy myself very important. I tried to listen to the wizard's instructions but was distracted by the transparency of the floor. Beneath our feet, the translucent ice revealed large sea-mammals chasing each other playfully. A large manatee even smiled up at me. My feet now freezing from the contact with the ice, I tried to tuck them under me in the armchair, but to no avail.

~

Stupid cold feet. I sat up and spread the duvet out neatly, folding it over the edge of the bed. I tucked my icy feet into the fold. 7:12am. I plunged back into unconsciousness.

~

Our carriage swerved at a blinding speed over the bridge and into the dark forest. It was definitely a horse-drawn carriage, with large wooden wheels and bales of hay and soft cushions as seating. But there were no horses. I sat crouched in the driver's seat, teetering precariously as the carriage raced along. I was aware of two women in the seats behind me but I was, for a moment, too

The Dream Story

distracted by the beauty and eeriness of the woods to pay attention to them. I finally swivelled around to find a white-haired old lady, clearly our leader, instructing the middle-aged woman next to her in the knitting of an odd-looking wool contraption. She caught my quizzical look and explained 'It's a magical net which releases the poisonous snakes during the battle'. I nodded. Best not be too inquisitive lest I be kicked out of my own dream.

In a blur the scene changed. We now stood in a wicker-decorated living room. The couple, whose house it was cowered in the corner, looking at the white-haired woman in fear. It seems we had barged into their home and were now demanding something of them. We were clearly very important people.

Under the old woman's instruction I found myself opening the top cabinet of a large cupboard. The woman spoke for the first time 'We don't fight anymore...' Our leader silenced her with a stare. I stared as well, trying to convey that I had some idea of what was going on. 'If you don't fight anymore, why is your equipment neatly folded in your living room cupboard?' the old lady almost spat out at them. She nodded towards the three wrapped turbans I had just pulled out of the cabinet. I started unravelling them, one white, one blue, one black. 'We don't fight anymore,' the woman repeated feebly, almost unsure of herself. The couple stood closely by each other. They took a step forward in unison. The woman wore white and the man a dark midnight blue, the exact same shades as the first two turbans. But who did the last one belong to? The woman seemed to read my mind; she hovered even closer, flanked by her husband. 'Our son...' she started. Her pause said it all. I felt almost sorry for them, forced to resume fighting after such a great loss. Our leader and the middle-aged woman started to exit, assured of their victory, followed by the reluctant couple. I fretfully attempted to fold the magic turbans back in the way I had found them. Come on, how were they wrapped? I would have to pay more attention if I didn't want people to discover I was a fraud and had not the slightest idea what was happening.

~

The alarm rang, a shrill unwelcome sound. 8am. I hit the snooze button. This dream was far too captivating to be interrupted by something as inconsequential as getting up for a lecture. Medieval literature, you'll just have to wait.

~

I climbed the sharp rocks. Cold waves lapped up at the bottom of the cliff below me. As I continued my ascent, cold gushes of wind started whipping me in the face, accompanied by drizzle. Must be Ireland. When I finally reached the top, I saw a supermarket, standing alone in the middle of a deserted plain. At the entrance, stood two policemen, one tall and thin, wearing a police bobby hat and a brown uniform, the other short, stout and bald, clad in a long green and beige chequered tweed coat. As I walked past I seemed to grasp that they were investigating the theft of their police dog. Suddenly I glimpsed my mother, pushing a trolley in the cereal aisle. I ran up to her, grateful for a familiar face, and asked her about Ireland, the steep cliff, the policemen and the oddly located supermarket. She interrupted my flow of questions. 'Shush, look for the round stickers', and she walked off, sliding her trolley along, flashing me a mischievous grin before disappearing behind the crisps. This was almost as weird as the knitted net of snakes.

I tried to exit the supermarket but the policemen stopped me: 'Excuse me miss, where are your stickers?' I looked up at them, perplexed. But my mother's words echoed in my head, and I returned to where I had last seen her. Sure enough on a box of Kellogg's, there it was, a green round sticker. On a nearby box I found a yellow one. I stuck them on my shirt and left the shop, this time ignored by the policemen, who had resumed their hushed whispering. The tall one had pulled out a magnifying glass and was inspecting it closely.

A swirly blur and I found myself in the passenger seat of a small Citroën 2CV. My mother was driving. 'Guess what?' she asked with a playful wink, and letting go of the steering wheel she reached into the booth. She pulled out a scruffy cocker spaniel who beamed happily at me and tried to lick my face. 'I stole their dog!' she announced triumphantly as we drove off along the cliff.

The Dream Story

~

8.10. Time to get up. Man that was an interesting night. I don't know what they put in that 'Cheese Please' pasta but I will definitely be having that *again. Might not tell anyone about these dreams though, they'll think I'm on hard drugs, or simply flying mad.*

The Exaphanisis
Agamemnon Apostolou

I: The Diplomat

Night Sun, 14 Aug 2011 – Mon, 15 Aug 2011
Panayotis, D. (Taxi driver)
I was driving down the ring road when I saw a line of smoke coming from the exit. I was worried for two seconds, until I presumed that it was the chimney of a provisional house. It didn't cross my mind until much later that the chimney smoke might have been on fire. Who could have thought of lighting his heating in the middle of the summer? By that time, I was already turning my car into the area I had been called to. For a moment I thought, it might be a bakery, baking bread for the following morning. Since I was working, I'd completely forgotten that it was a long-weekend-holiday
...

Knock. Knock. George Elias Walton looked at the door. His head was tired, trying to understand what had gone wrong all these days. Reading was one of the options which could help his understanding of what had happened the last few weeks in Thessaloniki, his current place of appointment as a consulate head of the United Kingdom.

He was reading the report given to him by the Greek police efforts to gain witnesses' accounts about the events of 15th August.

He had already read about forty witnesses, but they were all fragmented and unclear, and, mainly, too late. The last one he was reading, however, was the most accurate, probably because it was early enough, nearer to the moment when everything had started.

Unluckily, his office door was knocked just at the time he was reaching the crucial point. He was expecting someone, but surely not at four o'clock in the morning, just when the morning mist had started covering the clear starry sky of a beautiful Greek summer night.

Walton squeezed his eyes with both hands, gave a deep sigh, and cleared his throat.

Come in! ..." he said with this voice hoarse from exhaustion and a long week of consecutive nights of insomnia.

The door opened and a tall, blonde man entered the room. He was around his mid-thirties with a fair complexion and the slight impression of freckles on both of his cheeks indicating a skin sensitive to the summer light of Greece. He was wearing a summer suit –jacket, tie and a light-blue shirt– and polished shoes. His manner was very gentle and his step was confident and reassuring. His moves, behaviour and acts were subtle, precise – no move he made would be unnecessary, no word uttered, no smile formed would be over-expressive.

"Good morning, sir." His voice betrayed an English southern, high-class accent. "I apologise for the inappropriate time, but given the circumstances, you can understand we need to speed up some events."

"I, yes, absolutely, understand ... Besides, after that night no sleep has since found me easily, young man ..." responded Walton with a quiet voice.

"I'm Samuel Keaton. British Intelligence. I have come with the order by HM Government to relieve you from your post, Mr Walton. I suppose, however, you can give me a hand before, mister — ?"

"Absolutely. I'm fully aware of the duties, Mr Keaton. I am willing to help the service, if this is what you ask of me. Although I'd miss Greece, I can't wait for the time to leave it," said Walton with a tone of melancholy. "But, please, have a seat ... I can call the maid to serve us a cup of tea, if you wish. I'd rather have some coffee ..." said Walton, while he was starting to stand up.

"Mr Walton, I have ordered one vehicle to pick up your staff, daughter and wife and lead them to the airport, where they can get their flight to London, and another car where you and I can talk in private quietly", said Keaton seriously in a flat voice, in a matter-of-fact tone.

"A-all r-right," stuttered Walton, surprised by the readiness of Keaton and the Service.

"I will be waiting for you to get ready downstairs at the garage," added Keaton. He looked at his watch. "Shall we say we meet in about ninety minutes? Quarter to six, perhaps?"

II: Pointless

After saying goodbye to his family, Walton saw them entering the mini-bus leaving the mansion heading east towards the side of the airport.

Soon enough he found himself sitting on the back seat of a black Mercedes with Keaton. He could not see the driver because of the black glass wall dividing the front with the rear seats. Outside it was already morning and the bright light entered the vehicle lighting up the Nordic features of Keaton, which Walton had not noticed earlier in his dim-lit study.

"Mr Keaton, do you know where we are taking you?"

"I'm not sure, but I presume some kind of laboratory facility?"

"Not at all, the health checks you have all done the last few days indicate normal health conditions," replied Keaton slowly and quietly.

"So, what is it then?" asked Walton, getting a little impatient.

"Please be patient, Mr Walton. I know you've suffered a lot", said Keaton. "I just need some of your time, so that we can clarify what happened on the night of the events. Would you mind telling me your story?" he added and pulled out a fountain pen and a notepad from his case.

"Oh… Well, I've said it all before… To the press, to the Service, to the Government, to the Greeks…"

"It doesn't matter; what you have said, it is told. Please give me your account once more".

"Well… I was not in the city on the day. I had gone with my family to the country cottage in Halkidiki…" said Walton.

"The feast of the Virgin on Monday meant that we were going to have a long weekend, and all business and meetings in the city were postponed for the following days after the 16th August. On Monday night, the fifteenth, we headed home early before the traffic would increase by the people returning home. When I got into the city, I was indeed fascinated by the empty streets and roads, although it was somehow expected, since due to the holiday the Thessalonians tend to "flee" —so to speak. So, I had not thought — it didn't even cross my mind then, how could it?— that anything unusual might have occurred, let alone this!"

"When did you notice it, then?" asked Keaton flatly.

"Oh, well after that! The following morning I was planning to go to the consulate, and I decided to call the office secretary, who is my assistant, so that she would give me report of what happened over the couple of days I was in Halkidiki, before I was going to reach the office. I called at the office but still no one picked it up, hence I tried again and again, over three times... I wasn't worried... I thought the telephone lines might be out of order... Then I tried several times to call her mobile phone, as well as the colleagues from the other offices, but no one replied, so I thought it might've been the poor signal..."

Walton's voice faded. Pictures and sounds flooded his head. Words could not describe the incredible absurdity of such an experience.

He remembered.

Walton was sitting alone at the desk reflecting what had happened.

Where was everybody? he wondered suspiciously.

His thoughts stopped, as his wife's loud outburst was heard through the staircase from upstairs.

"George!"

Walton had hardly stood up when his wife entered his study.

"What is it, Henrietta?" he mumbled quietly.

Her look was obviously worried and showed marks of anxiety. Her strawberry-blonde-dyed hair showed the evident marks of sleep-time untidiness.

"Oh! George!" she cried.

The Exaphanisis

Walton moved towards her, while she sat down on the armchair in front of the desk with a blank look on her face. He looked at her and the state of her sleepiness emphasised the lines of ageing on her alabaster skin, which Walton had not noticed before. An irrelevant wave of affection for his wife overwhelmed him, reinforced by a flash of memories of thirty-five years of happy marriage.

He sat down opposite her and asked her quietly:
"What happened — ?"

"Mr Walton?"
Walton came back from his reverie. The light from the window showed that it was well into morning by now. The fatigue of five consecutive days of insomnia made him feel quite ill and it was difficult to focus. Keaton realised this but he continued.

"Mr Walton, please be patient for a little longer. Please tell me, when did you realise what had happened?"

"By noon, I had already had a full picture of the situation. I mean, there had been rumours all morning, you know, television broadcasts, calls from neighbours. You see, many presumed, as I had thought in the beginning, that it was a telephone network issue — who could dare believe that something collective happened to everybody in the city?

"But by noon, the city had been visited by many, and they'd already seen that telephones worked fine", added Walton. "Then, the Greek authorities came to me and told me. On Wednesday, of course, came the formal governmental announcement..."

"On Tuesday, had many returned to the city from their long weekend excursions?" asked Keaton gently.

"Precisely. They were shocked to find the streets empty, too. On a working day? Who could believe ... ?"

Walton stopped. His voice was tired and hoarse; his mouth dry; he wanted to go. With extreme difficulty, he gathered his remaining power and said:

"Mr Keaton, I'm exhausted. I terribly need to rest. I've told you everything I know..."

Keaton realised that he had reached Walton's limit.

"All right, Mr Walton. I'll tell the chauffeur to drive you safely home — I won't need you any longer..." said Keaton with a casual kindness. "Just one more question?...

"I believe the Greek police have given you records of witnesses' accounts, isn't that right?"

"Indeed so!... There they are", said Walton who was unexpectedly holding the folder he was reading earlier firmly in his hand. He passed it to Keaton, who took it with a serious interest. Keaton called a man who ushered Walton towards the car park. He looked at the sunny blue sky with a faint smile. The breeze hit his face and he already felt better.

"Nice place..." he murmured. He would miss it. At least he would go home.

III. The Britons

Keaton glanced at the shabby folder. He had read hundreds of reports over the last a few days, but none of them was adequately concise or near the time of the events. Fragmented pieces and bites of accounts hours after dawn. Limited information for one of the most important events of the twenty-first century, perhaps. He browsed through the folder that the consulate had given him.

Documents, interviews with witnesses. A fine mess on its own, reinforced by the untidiness of the Greek police. Probably that folder was as useful as the rest he had read. However, he hoped that this time he would find something on the morning of the events. It was the transcriptions from the police interrogation. The time was good! It was the earliest that Keaton had seen until now! He enthusiastically sat up in his seat and read hungrily.

Night Sat, 13 Aug 2011 – Sun, 14 Aug 2011
Panayotis, D. (Taxi driver)
I was driving down the ring road when I saw a line of smoke coming from the exit. I was worried for two seconds, until I presumed that it was the chimney of a provisional house. It didn't cross my mind until much later that the chimney smoke might have been on fire. Who could have thought of lighting his heating in the

middle of the summer? By that time, I was already turning my car into the area I had been called to. For a moment I thought, it might be a bakery, baking bread for the following morning. Since I was working, I'd completely forgotten that it was a long-weekend-holiday.

I drove into the street I was called to for a pick-up. There was dead silence. It was the crack of dawn. My client was not there, but I didn't get worried — most of them are normally late. I didn't hit the horn, because it was still rather early, so I called the number I was given. In retrospect, now I believe I could hear their phone ringing through the window.

Nobody picked it up. I thought they were on their way down. Maybe they had overslept. I turned on the radio while waiting for them. But all the stations broadcasted a loud static, so I switched it off… I went out of my car to stretch a little and lit a cigarette. It was dead quiet and I thought it was normal, because it was a holiday. I smoked my cigarette when I realised that the smoke I was smelling was not that of my smoking. I looked around and it was getting brighter and brighter but I noticed a flicker of light at the end of the road.

"What the hell?" I said, because it looked as if it were a big fire and it smelled like burnt tyres and oil. I walked down the road and turned left, which was the way to the main street. Then, my jaw dropped. There was a large lorry fully aflame (!), crashed at the corner of a street, right at the bend of the street. Four other cars were also crashed!

One car had smashed through the front window of a grocery shop. The second had overturned a kiosk. The third had climbed on two parked cars, whereas the fourth one was divided into two, having smashed into an electricity pole.

I started swearing. The fire of the lorry was climbing up the block of flats and soon the whole building — it seemed to me— would turn into ashes!

Spontaneously, I took my mobile from my pocket and called the fire brigade. Instead of the typical beeping, however, I got the "occupied-call" sound. Then

I tried the police. Still nothing. Then, I thought my phone was out of order.

"What the hell?" I said. "No one available?" In a matter of seconds, I was shouting out loud. It was a densely populated neighbourhood. Someone would come out and help. The silence really gave me the creeps. The fire was becoming bigger spreading to the five-story building.

I shouted again. No reply. And then it hit me.

I saw no car, no pedestrian in the high street. It was early morning and everything, but then at least someone must be walking down the street and I rang all the doorbells of every flat. No reply. I was shocked. No reaction? Where was everybody? A sudden massive plague? Everybody on holiday? *Everybody?...*

With this thought, I ran to the next block of flats and then the next one, but I received no reply. I was looking around, while the fire was now consuming the whole building. I ran quietly to the smashed cars, to see whether the drivers were there. I had the feeling I would not find any drivers and I was right. No bodies, no injured. No soul moving down the street. I looked around to the end of the street.

I saw something even more unbelievable: a series of cars smashed left and right all along the main street. Other cars were stalled in the middle of the street with the keys in the ignition.

A long bus had crashed on a pavement tree. Anywhere I looked there were signs of sudden abandonment and, of course, no people to see. I thought I was having a dream. I was pinching myself trying to wake up, you know, how it feels... As if you are in a dream...

Keaton had read enough. An interesting account, of course, yet full of subjectivities and generalities. And it was too late, still. He wanted an even earlier account, for most of the things he had now read were known. He sat pensively trying to reflect on what he had read. The strong morning sun was entering the small window of the room. It was getting hot. While he was standing up, in order to exit the room, a short knock at the door was heard and a man of his age entered the room.

It was Christian Backhouse. He was his associate for his mission, although he was a little older in the Service. He was a medium-height dark-haired man, with pointy nose and jaw. He wore a pair of small spectacles and a summer black suit. In contrast to Keaton, Backhouse was a more outspoken, outgoing and sociable character, very good with women, even if he was not extremely good looking.

"In my opinion, I think you work too much", Backhouse said with a faint hint of sarcasm.

Keaton felt annoyed.

"What would you have me do, mister? Let me sleep, while time passes by?"

"I say, you get tired of doing too much while achieving too little in return. I'm not judging you! I'm just trying to advise you… Be productive! Don't do too much for too little!" said Backhouse with a faint smile. He obviously wanted to tease Keaton.

Keaton realised this, feeling a little more annoyed. He was working all night, while Backhouse could sleep in peace and now he was joking about him!

"I've been reading the reports, if you want to know! What've *you* been doing, your Highness?" reacted Keaton.

Backhouse stared back directly towards his friend's eyes, while smiling sarcastically.

"What — ?" asked Keaton, obviously irritated. "Is there any news, or what?"

Backhouse flipped the folder's documents, which Keaton had just read, with his thumb. He sat on the desk and said without looking at him:

"We've got your taxi driver, he's right here with us. The Greek police are very eager to inform us about the movements of our compatriots. You see the first thing they told me was that they gave these copies of transcription to our consulate. So, I took one more copy. You see… our Service has means of persuasion…"

"Where's the taxi driver?"

"Oh! Just upstairs!…" said Backhouse casually. "Very irritable. He seemed as though he didn't like to be taken from bed at four o'clock in the morning! He's constantly shouting about rights and liberties!" he added ironically.

"Maybe I should talk to him!…"

"Of course, you will — you are the best with Greek in the Service! But don't get excited — I have bad news for you, as well!"

"What is it?"

"It's America. They are here and they want to talk to you".

Keaton swore.

"Yeah… We gotta deal with the big boys now, buddy!" Backhouse said with a fake American accent.

"What do they want?" asked Keaton.

"What we want, of course. They've just got the means to acquire it!"

"Damn!" exclaimed Keaton. "What does London say?"

"The same old stuff!…" replied Backhouse. "To achieve the highest level of cooperation. Support and help our best ally!"

Keaton sighed. Why did he have to abide to the rules of partnership and lose his autonomy to this? It was expected logic that the Americans are here, he thought. He should not be surprised. He had better abandon his professional selfishness and conform to the headquarters' guidelines. Cooperation… Why not? Perhaps, this would be good. Besides, maybe the Americans could give them a hand at the end.

"OK. Call them in. I'll speak to them now." he ordered. "And then bring the Greek here, to speak with him all together."

Backhouse exited the room and went to bring the people in.

Keaton sat on the chair trying to think what he would tell them. He had to say everything yet again.

Everything that had happened.

IV. Flashback

The 14th August 2011 was a normal day for Thessaloniki. The second largest city of Greece, home of nearly a million souls, looked like mirror under the burning Greek summer sun. Life was slow due to the peak of the holiday season and the great religious feast of the following day. Many of the city's inhabitants had been away due to

The Exaphanisis

the festival of the Dormition of the Virgin on the following day.[1] As the sun set behind the western mountains across the calm waters of the Thermaic Gulf, nothing seemed to betray any disturbance in the calmness of the evening. During the evening dusk boat bars sailed on their pleasant short cruises around the Gulf.

Night time. Manos was drinking from a bottle of icy cold beer. He and his friend were sitting on two wooden chairs on the balcony discussing quietly, enjoying the light suburban night breeze.

"Definitely, we need change, man!" his friend Alexis exclaimed. "Either from the Left or the Right, this state needs change!"

"It's pity how the brought they country into this, anyway!" said Manos disappointed. "Elections might be reasonable, but wouldn't that bring instability?"

"Democracy needs risks", affirmed Alexis.

"With any costs?" questioned Manos.

"Anyway, I can't believe this will bring change, anyway... International pressure... The Americans... The Europeans... All put their hand into it."

"That is true!... But how can *we* do better as a nation?" wondered Manos.

"The bloody traitors! Who knows? We'll see what is gonna happen soon", said Alexis while having a sip of his bottle.

Manos sighed and looked at his watch. Quarter to three.

"It's nearly three, man! I'd better get going..." said Manos.

"No! Come on, stay man! It's not uni time now! You can sleep here. My parents are away, you can leave in the morning..." said Alexis.

"I'm afraid I can't. We're going to the village to see grandma. We'll be leaving early in the morning. I can hardly get some sleep until my mum will be knocking my door violently next morning", said Manos jokingly.

"OK man! As you wish", replied Alexis. "See you soon!"

"See you, boy! Happy holiday!"

"You too, man! You too!"

---

1 Corresponds to the Assumption of the Virgin

Manos walked down the stairs, across the small garden and down to his scooter motorcycle. He put on his helmet and put his hand in his shorts' pockets, but he could not find his keys.

"Where the hell are they?" he said out aloud.

He saw Alexis coming out of the garden holding Manos's keys.

"Did you forget those?" Alexis said. "They were left on the balcony table".

"Thanks, mate!"

They said goodnight to each other again. Alexis entered back into his house. Manos looked at his watch. Five past three. Damn! He was late.

He climbed on his scooter, put the engine on and drove outside the village moving towards the exit to the motorway. The way was clear; traffic was low. People were either already away on holiday or sleeping to leave the next day.

The scooter entered the motorway. In twenty minutes, Manos calculated, he would be at the city entrance, which meant that he needed ten more minutes to be in bed at home.

He was three kilometres behind the assumed city entrance, which was at the IKEA complex, where the bus routes started. It must be around twenty to four, Manos thought, while the wind was hitting his chest. A fast white van overtook him fast, making a loud roar of its engine.

Where does this guy think he's going like this? Manos thought angrily, mostly because the loud engine had frightened him.

His gaze followed the van which had now passed the IKEA complex, when the most unexpected thing happened.

A white light, like a lightning, emerged out of nowhere amid the cloudless black night sky with a light so strong that Manos quickly closed his eyes. A second later, while he was still driving, the light was gone.

What was that? Manos thought. For a moment he worried that he was asleep, while driving. He saw that, didn't he?

His gaze was still looking ahead. The white van was off course moving fast out of the motorway and eventually it crashed loudly into the wall of a large warehouse.

Manos gasped. The stupid guy! He was going so fast! The crash looked severe. Manos stopped just two or three meters behind the crashed van at the pavement and got off his scooter. He placed his helmet on the scooter seat and moved quickly over to the crashed van.

The crash was severe. The whole front was smashed violently into half its length. Manos moved toward the driver's window to check on the condition of the driver. The windows were closed and intact. Manos looked inside.

Surprisingly, there was no driver. The seatbelt was sealed, the airbag had been activated, but the driver was nowhere. The light blue light of dawn was helping him to see better. He opened the door and looked more thoroughly inside the driver's cabin. The cool air that touched his face made him realise that the windows were closed because the air conditioning had been on. But where was the driver? And, if the windows were intact, how did he come out?

Manos looked back at the motorway. No car had passed yet. He looked around. No body, no man walking nearby. The morning twilight was enlightening the landscape of a soulless environment.

He immediately called the emergency service. No response. Damn! Was that time for his mobile to be out of order?

While he was calling in vain and simultaneously looking at the motorway, a car approached and Manos waved at it. The car pulled over and a middle-aged man with a thick mouse-grey moustache came out.

"Are you OK, son? Did you crash? Are you hurt?"

"No! I came with the scooter!" exclaimed Manos. "The driver's not in the seat! I can't find him! I saw him crashing, but I didn't find him!"

"What?" the man said. He approached the van opened the door and looked inside. "Where has the damn driver been, then?"

"I've no clue, sir! He must've been thrown out of the car somehow!" said Manos, while still vainly trying to call the emergency service number. "Sir, do you have a mobile phone? I can't reach the police or the ambulance!"

"Yes, of course!" said the man. He tried. No reply. "And then we call ourselves a state!" he said angrily. "No reply. These buggers ain't operational!"

"Do you want to go and call for help? There is an Express Service branch. They must be open even today, sir? Do you want to go and call them to come here?"

"You'd better go yourself!" said the man kindly. "You have the scooter and you know better where it is".

Manos agreed and quickly drove away to the Express Service. The yellow flickers of sun were seen behind the mountains at the East.

The scooter entered the city boroughs. He moved in through empty streets, when suddenly he saw cars stalled in the middle of the street. Cars smashed at the corner of every block. Fires from smashed cars and broken windows. No people walking. Yet the most striking were the cars stalled and abandoned in the middle of the streets.

Abandoned. That is how the whole city looked like.

Manos was so shocked that he never stopped on his route driving towards the Express Service. He reached it and got off quickly. He saw that the light was on and his heart jumped with excitement. He pushed the unlocked door and ran to the garage.

"Anybody here?" he shouted.

No reply.

"Hello! Anybody here?" he tried again — in vain.

"ANYBODY?!" he screamed.

The only reply was an echo.

Now his mind flew home. Home...

"Damn!" he exclaimed.

He jumped on the scooter.

He drove fast. He ignored the traffic lights, zigzagging between the stalled cars.

He reached home. He entered the lift. First... Second... Third... Fourth floor!

The keys! Quickly!

He entered his home. Suitcases packed and ready waiting next to the door. He moved into his sister's room. Pushed the door. She was not there! He felt as if he could never swallow again. He ran to his parents' bedroom. He opened the door ajar!

No one was there either.

He ran off to the scooter. He drove like a mad man towards the city centre. Always the same abandoned scenery.

V. The Americans

"So, Mr Keaton…" said Roger Miller. "The problem is the disappearance of people."

"If you put it bluntly, yes," replied Keaton coldly.

They were sitting under the shadow of pine trees at the backyard of the small house.

"The reason you are here, Mr Keaton, is this", said Miller calmly. His white face seemed to be as sensitive to the sun as Keaton's. Behind him, like bodyguards, a black and a white agent were standing nearby listening passively to the conversation. "The US Administration wishes to know what caused the problem, Mr Keaton…"

"I told you everything, I know, Mr Miller", said Keaton coldly. "I've got nothing to hide."

"Of course…" said Miller casually. "Our special relationship. I know London would have no reservation to *cooperate*. Right, Mr Keaton?"

Keaton felt his stomach shrinking, but he let no facial expression reveal this.

"We appreciate our alliance", affirmed Keaton.

"Precisely!" said Miller with a sudden excitement. "So do we, my friend!" He snapped his fingers and the black man behind him drew a tablet computer from his pocket and gave it to him.

"Since your worthless efforts to extract useful information from stupid taxi drivers, I've got something to show to the both of you…"

Keaton stood up, his head heated up and red with rage.

"I see no reason whatsoever to be offensive, *sir*! If this is the policy that the Administration is following…"

"Calm down, Sam!" whispered Backhouse.

"Why don't you both shut up and have a look at this?" said Miller bluntly. He gave them the tablet, while the video was showing.

It was footage from a CCTV camera. It was the early hours of day of the Event: 15-08-2011, 04:41. The camera showed the panoramic view of a garage with three people working what seemed to be a routine shift. At the end, one could see the street and the pavement lit by a weak street lamp, it was still night.

04:44. The same routine. Suddenly, a bright light out of nowhere made the video show a completely white screen. That lasted no more than two seconds. Then the image blackened, as if the camera had turned off and it came back to life immediately. When the image was clear enough to see again, the boys were not there. The garage was empty. No move. Just the street lamp's yellowish colour.

"That footage is taken by a 24/7 CCTV camera of a motorway emergency company called Express Service", said Miller. "It shows the exact moment of the so-called *Event* with great accuracy".

"Yeah, but ..." whispered Backhouse.

"Keep watching", said the American.

The video time lapsed. A stray dog passed by in fast motion. Of course, Keaton recalled, animals were unaffected. The morning light penetrated the garage. The street lamp was turned off. The time lapse stopped. A scooter motorcycle parked just outside the garage. A twenty-year-old man came into view. He was moving fast and was obviously in a hurry. He seemed to have been looking for something. Suddenly, he jumped back to his scooter and left. The video stopped.

"Yeah..." said Backhouse. "I don't see what we can get out of this — "

"Of course!" said Miller. "But *we* can! And *we* have, Mr Bauhaus!"

"Backhouse!" Backhouse breathed out angrily. He clenched his fists tightly.

"Yes, yes!" said Miller. "This man you just saw was most probably one of the first ten who entered the city. He was just about ten minutes in the garage after that *White Light*. We traced him, we know who he is."

"How?..." said Backhouse.

"The scooter's number plates, dummy!" interrupted Keaton. He blinked at Backhouse discreetly. He did not want his team to be exposed again to the American.

"I see, you are getting it now!" smiled Miller ironically. "London will be so proud, when we tell them that their kids have learnt to read!"

It was fortunate that Backhouse was standing behind Keaton, otherwise he would have happily jumped to strangle Miller.

VI. Dreamlike Fantasy

"This is a bad dream…"

Manos awoke. Four days. Four days in a ghost city. His parents gone, most of his friends lost. The Government even more lost — metaphorically speaking—, more than ever, already incompetent in its own right.

On Wednesday afternoon, 17 August 2011, the Greek government had announced that the city of Thessaloniki missed nearly one million souls. By a supernatural, incomprehensible phenomenon, the people of the city disappeared mysteriously in a matter of seconds.

"For thirty-five hours, the communications with the armed forces, the police, the fire brigade were out of order, but no one confirmed what was happening. With great regret and great agony, we declare that approximately eight hundred thousand people in Thessaloniki have been missing since Monday morning and no explanation of reasonable mind can give us a clear account for what has happened", said the Prime Minister in his speech.

The subsequent complications, of course, were enormous! Many of the people of Thessaloniki were away for the holiday. About a hundred thousand returned from holiday, finding an abandoned city. That also went against the plans of the Government to implement a military regime in the Thessaloniki area and evacuate the city. Rumours said that the country's economic crisis could be solved by liquidating the assets of the people missing. They were not dead, but they were nowhere to be found. Moral, political and legal arguments and interests collided.

The first two days were, as if no one had realised anything. At least no one official.

Soon groups of people from outside the city, local villagers, caravans of Gypsies, even people crossing the border from the neighbouring countries flocked into the city. Looting. Hundreds of flats unguarded, forgotten. Besides, there was no one to miss anything, if something was stolen.

The police consisting of police officers from all over the country, mainly from Athens and neighbouring towns, were still fighting in vain to contain crime of such an unprecedented level.

Manos had hidden his scooter. He did not believe it would be stolen, there were thousands of those all around for everyone to steal, but he wanted to keep it safe, just in case. Sometimes he left his flat quietly on foot. He stayed in the city, despite the repetitive invitations of Alexis and his family, because he wanted to make sure his home would be safe from looting. He stayed indoors, mostly. But sometimes he needed to do "shopping".

Manos liked "shopping". He called it euphemistically "hunting". It was more or less sensible looting. He went to his neighbourhood mini market, whose windows was broken by the previous looters, and took basic products he would need for survival, mostly food. He then normally returned home quietly, without anyone finding out.

His neighbourhood was normally quiet. The looters could be heard sometimes, but mostly they tended not to approach his street. Sometimes he left the street with his scooter to browse the empty city. One day he stole petrol from a station near his home. The loss of his parents and sister was so distant and surreal that he did not really feel sad. He was actually excited. Everything seemed like a dream, as if he was experiencing a dreamlike fantasy, in which he could roam in an empty city with his scooter taking any food or product from the shops for free.

He wanted to do some "hunting" and get some fresh air away from the claustrophobic feeling of staying home listening to the pointless discussions of Athenian politicians. No one felt the desert of this ghost city. Words, promises, lies, lies. And panic. Panic. Panic that war was happening, the Martians were invading, the

Russians were coming, the Americans, the Jews, the Antichrist, the global elite. A logical reaction, perhaps, yet it was sheer panic.

Manos walked back home when he saw three men in MIB suits pressing his apartment's doorbell. He swore. He hid himself behind the street corner. Who are these people looking for him? He felt like the hero of a bad Hollywood film. He ran to the back alley, where he had hidden his scooter. He pushed it slowly towards the street, when one of the men looked at him and screamed.

"Here! He's here!"

Manos felt his heartbeat speeding by the adrenaline. He turned the engine on and hit the gas. The scooter flew away as fast as it could.

The men got in their black cars and started chasing him. *Me?* Manos wondered. *Why me?*

He drove carelessly, zigzagging to avoid the stalled cars, hoping to confuse his pursuers. He entered the ring road. Mistake, he thought. That bloody scooter could not go over a hundred kilometres per hour! The men-in-black would catch him!

The sound from the sky brought him back to reality. This is a dream! It can't be true! A helicopter was hovering ten metres above his head. A guy in a megaphone shouted at him.

"Manos! Stop now! Get off the motorbike! Put your hands behind your head!"

Manos's jaw dropped. He pulled over on the corner of the motorway, while three black cars surrounded him cyclically. This is too much! He smiled, unable to believe himself being in such a position. He did as instructed.

VII. Caught

Handcuffed hands behind the back.

He was pushed inside a stuffy room. They took his handcuffs off. He was escorted to a comfortable backyard, where they placed him to sit.

A blonde man approached him. He wore a disgusting smile, which he immediately recognised as fake.

"Mr Tsakos," he told him. "Apologies for all this inconvenience. I am Samuel Keaton. You can call me Sam, if you want."

Manos could tell by his name that he was a foreigner, despite his almost impeccable accent.

"How can I help you?" said Manos in a straightforward manner.

"Wait! Would you like some juice? Tea? Coffee?" asked Keaton.

"No, thanks..." replied Manos. "What have I done? What is my crime?" Manos was worried that his trivial "hunting" was what had caused him all of this trouble.

"No — nothing — no crime..." said Keaton. And he told him about what they needed, a simple interrogation, that's all.

Manos felt little reassured, but still aloof.

"What is it, then?"

Keaton asked him if he remembered anything about the night of the Event.

Manos's heart felt much lighter. It was not about his "hunting".

He told him about the van crash and the Express Service.

"Before these!... Did you see any white light?" asked Keaton seriously.

"Light!... No!... Er... Now that you mention it, yeah!... Of course! It was as if a lightning was struck and the whole city was in white, but just for a second or so. It was so unreal that it almost slipped my mind!" exclaimed Manos.

Keaton thanked him and stood up.

"You are dismissed, Mr Tsakos," said Keaton. "The door over there will lead you outside. You may go. Thank you. Oh! One more thing... What is your age?"

"I'm twenty years old."

"Great! Well done. Thank you!"

"Do you think this *Light* was what caused all this, Mr Keaton?"

"Everything is possible in this world," replied Keaton flatly.

VIII. Escape

Manos walked along the sandy beach. How unreal was all this! He wanted to wake up from the absurdities of this "dream". He thought that, perhaps, his family had woken up now, preparing to leave for their trip to grandma's and he was the one still asleep.

Everything is possible in this world. Keaton's voice echoed in his mind. Perhaps, if he fell into the water he would wake up in the real world by the shock.

Perhaps...

Three First Pages of Unwritten Novels
David Lowry

Across the Way

In-between poetry and ruminating upon Proust, half incompleted plays, reveries of women's forms, unbound fragments of film footage and watering the small tree on the windowsill, there was a man I often saw. I saw him often enough. I saw him dressed in the dark polo-neck and scarf of night: he came only when the hours hushed and the street-cars tamed and the myriad walkers bedded down in each others' homes: he was there.

In between a chasm, the walls of which were complex, uneven bricks, framed tight as an iris in the window-frame he leant. And yet he drew upon the cigarettes and leant, his arms in rags, on his chin and head, a hat. He leant, bent low upon the windowsill across the high and narrow Cornwall Rd.

I saw him there each night, though I didn't look up at his hidden virile eyes of thought, and never had I thought till then that every night he emerged out the hatch, drenched in earth. And sometimes he was filthy, or soaked, or singed and smouldered, or bald and stubbled, or long, languid and set away out somewhere in the night. His ruin changed and merged and worsened each day, and sometimes he was gone from my sight altogether: out in the wide, wide jungles of somewhere.

And so, one night, when his hat fell into the street and blew away, I called upon him from across the way and enquired of his being, his shape, his hearth. And among the silence of the city streets far below he awoke and spoke and told me why. The many things he spoke to me! From within his ravaged and coughing sea: an ocean, a mire of thoughts and things that you would *never* tell to any man across the way. We peeked into a distant life like an instigation of the morning's promises of day: because I was a whole world and sixty feet away, because I was there in this world and somehow without: he told me his mysteries, long, long after my cigar had gone out.

He raised his head. He looked up to the faraway pin-tips of our eyes. I listened then, the way one listens for the setting of a gun.

***

He had a woman, he said: a woman curved like the arch of the morning, curved and ripe like a drinking cat's back. This was three and a half years before. He went on.

And When I Looked Long into the Dark of my Own Days

And when I looked back, long into the dark of my own days: was I afraid then? I looked deep and, for a while, going through the thundering forest, lit from the lamplight of the flickered moon, I looked far into the long dark of my own days: and as the air charged with chiming electric, as the air clears into total floating clarity, as it does before it heaves a year's weight in rain, I looked long into the dark of my own days and yet-- I was afraid.

***

Beats fell like wine out the hands of us mean men into the air, into the wind and then to the earth again. And I was an old tailor in the dusty spaces of time past: going along, opening our way through the cavern of dusk, that's waiting at the eulogy of a day. The Shoeworker had no complaints because the Salesman had them all, and begged us through a horse understanding to stop going along this way and camp, yet the Raven Merchant, the Horseshoe Robber, the Galley Cook, the Tinker and the Tailor listened and ignored him while they thought of women and walked alone. I could hear the pots and pans unwashed. I could hear the shoes' drying leather. I could hear our cogs turning on some quiet matter and the Raven Merchant cooing a faraway pigeon into sight.

If you could see us when we leaned and stopped walking, a rest one of many. If you hid behind a rock above us, and peeped: an old half of a harp was being played above the passing water, in and out, the mappy looked up and the sky looked down and bent beneath a rock in doubt for.

'Two more miles isn't far enough; we'll take the night, that'll be enough.'

And he got us up and left for more. Our walkers walked a long, long walk to a tall, slim inn, staggering: and bent down by the window and passed through dinner and mead while the rain hadn't come, and stayed still in the roof of the forest. The Tinker paid by promise and a few odd-job rewinds on the high-up thatch: he descended slowly and so we left; deeper into our days, deep more. A pall of tread-marks o'er the floor we left.

Twenty miles on our strange paces caught up to us, our solemn pensive faces, dripping, turned a colour sylvan of the trees: the Raven Merchant was in another place than we were, it seemed: the merchant was somewhere not to be seen. The Raven Merchant was nowhere to be seen: we bent our legs unto the earth and sat and thought, ruminated. The Tinker, poor man, asked me then: was I the last one to see him? I was, I had, deep in the night.

An Island Off Bayonne

In an island off Bayonne, the Weather-Shapers waste their days with leaning on trees and amateur theatre plays. Within this isle off Bayonne there is a boat that for long you've known about. Far beyond the shores there nestles a ship, stranded comfortably: and on it there is known to be a deck, a mast and a horn turned South, into a gramophone, into a denizen of forgotten arias, or hidden arias... Amidst the tea-tree smoke, the mist arose from glades unbound, the steaming of the funnel was turned North, into a coffee-kettle: and yet, among the wind that bent trees away from the sun, and hid them, we are in the midst of life. Life most divine and treacherous. And, as you know already-- wasted. The Weather-Shapers drink the days like bourbon smoothie shakes.

On the ship, in the little island off Bayonne, trouble brews below the enclosing canopy. Phorea, it must be said, will screw just about anything: and that's her trouble, or so thinks her double, her partner, the Captain, the father of the ship (her brother but they've forgotten about that). He wears a hat and a telescope on his hip, under a belt of vines, under a pelt of stars enclosing, he finds her ever more and more enticing. But hey, what are men for? Some time on the apse, and sometimes on the fore (and mostly on the floor) is the loser's hero, Tulandro: and he wears a beard of tiredness that's stuck with oil and kerosene. He boards beneath the deck and is the keeper of the light, the only left: he peeks above the deck through a hole in her floor... that's what he does beneath the deck... and yawns.

Philodendron is a lass the stalk forgot: she was late, he sent the penguin instead, *he* was late – she was born at 23 to a hopeless family. Hopeless is what you are after you wait for that long. She dozes on the beach and droops of John, who sails by in the flood, which rises like a bath full when ev'ry night-time comes. He keeps people out and others in: he's the baron of the wind: he sleeps within a trunk on the starboard bough. Dormeer sleeps in the crow's nest: and she's in love with John, John with Elena who no one's mentioned yet, Philodendron with the Captain, the Captain Phorea and Philo (a shy and lascivious man), Elena with the worldly earth and Dormeer with the sea (and John, as you know already). Whoever's left is just fine on their own.

Each night as the river rises through the isle off sleep-drought Bayonne, the Weather-Shapers and the Weather-Geats, who dwell someplace underground, create the weather for the world with their hands and air and levers, and have been doing so pretty well much forever. But, as I've said, and as you already know: trouble is brewing on the sloshing sea bed, trouble rolling in the undertow.

***

It was night-time when, on a little isle of Bayonne, the crop came: the apples fell, and the work stopped before it began. What do we have here? Glimpses of swaying hips as Phorea drags in several tiger corpses on chains. Coughs as Tulandro smokes far out into the East, catching sleeping finches and various herbs and sleeps shhusshes as Dormeer creates her specialist tea from bark and tar and feathers from the sky (and some from Tulandro's pouches). Squawkings as Philodendron puts her shoes on backwards, blessed girl, through her doleful eye (the Captain's leant eye-patch). Nothing: for the Weather-Geats beat their feet and sweet their mead with the worker bees. Nothing again: as rain comes down upon the prow, the Captain stands, not at sea, not proud, he rains on himself and harbours long the dreadful wish: to be a tiger dead and dished, to be upon Phorea's fingertips. He cocks his hat and steers the ship.

Sweet dream harmless tunes, deciphered from Atlantic runes, play from John's wine-flute: ring around the finger clinking on the stem, clanging on the anchor he steadies himself, and gives the look of being all by himself. His Elena is in shadows, faraway though, he says himself. Half the island's set on fire and everyone wraps in baroque attire, while Tulandro calms the fire he made with libations of absinthe: the Captain frowns and chucks his sorrow-rain o'er the whole isle. Philo' wonders and kinks a sultry eye to someone standing nearby. The fire goes back unto the earth: Tulandro goes back to mirth. The flood swamps down from up high: Phor'a dances in the Captain's old misery-rain: dogs and foxes on the planes, cats and felines on parade.

The table John made from his boat is set: London's dry while on an island off Bayonne, the wine fills up with drips and drups, and the diners dine, getting wet. All eyes turn upon each other: sons and daughters, lampshades, beasts and brothers. Through the mist and the tea and the jungled human heat, move seven pairs of enamoured feet: and trouble brews itself down beneath. The table shakes the sky.